A MATTER
OF TRUST

BY

PENNY JORDAN

MILLS & BOON LIMITED
ETON HOUSE   18-24 PARADISE ROAD
RICHMOND   SURREY   TW9 1SR

CHAPTER ONE

'BUT Leigh, *you're* the private detective, not me,' Debra pointed out firmly to her stepsister. 'I'm a tax accountant.'

'A tax accountant who is just about to start a week's holiday and who doesn't have to attend a business meeting that's vital to her business,' Leigh interrupted quickly.

Although there were six years between them and Leigh was the elder, it had always been Debra who had been the calm, down-to-earth one, and Leigh the impulsive cause of family chaos.

'Look, Debs, you *know* how important this business is to me,' Leigh pleaded coaxingly now. 'After Paul left me, after the divorce, I felt as though my whole life was over. Now, since Jen and I started up Secrets, I feel as though life actually has some proper purpose again. I wouldn't ask you to help if there were anything difficult or dangerous involved. It's simply a matter of spending a few days in an empty house, keeping a tape-recorded list of someone's comings and goings, that's all.

'He won't even know you're there. We've persuaded his next-door neighbour to go and visit her sister so that we can use her house. I promise you, you won't have to do a thing other than——'

'Keep a twenty-four hour surveillance over someone's cheating husband,' Debra interrupted drily. 'Look, Leigh, I disapprove of men who cheat on their wives and families just as much as you do, but——'

'This one isn't cheating on his wife,' Leigh told her flatly, her normally animated face suddenly set hard. 'He's trying to seduce a seventeen-year-old into leaving home and going to live with him... He's thirty-four, Debs, with a string of women in his past and a taste for innocent young girls.' Her mouth tightened in distaste.

'According to her mother, Ginny is completely besotted with him and won't listen to a thing either of her parents has to say. They felt if they could present her with concrete evidence of the kind of man he really is, although it will hurt her now, it will save her much more pain in the long run.

'She's a clever girl, Debs, university material, with her whole life ahead of her, but this man has a reputation for picking up and discarding clever young girls like her.'

Debra sighed. She could feel herself weakening. And was it really so much that Leigh was asking? She knew what a struggle her stepsister had had since her marriage broke up. Deserted by her husband and with two small children to support, she had changed overnight from a bright, breezy, bubbly personality into a withdrawn, tormented woman whom Debra barely recognised.

But since she and a friend had set up this detective agency specialising in handling cases mainly for other women she had recovered all her lost self-esteem. The business, although moderately successful, was still quite precariously balanced and very much in its infancy. With her partner away on a much-needed short holiday and Leigh herself suddenly being offered the opportunity to expand into a wider market, Debra could quite understand why Leigh should feel it was so essential that she not miss out on this all-important meeting.

Equally she could also understand why, having organised events so that a twenty-four-hour watch could be kept on the man involved in this current case, Leigh was pleading with her to take her place in the next-door house and watch him for her.

'You won't have to keep watch on him for the full twenty-four hours,' Leigh was telling her coaxingly now. 'I've arranged for Jeff to watch the house from midnight to seven in the morning from a car outside.'

Jeff was Leigh's boyfriend, a solid, placid man, a teacher, some fifteen years older than Leigh, whom Debra liked and thought an ideal partner for her more volatile stepsister.

'Look, I wouldn't ask you if I weren't absolutely desperate,' Leigh told her. 'The parents are going to have the girls for me, but you're the only person...'

'Soft enough to be persuaded into helping you out,' Debra finished drily for her. 'All right,' she agreed, adding under her breath, 'I just hope I don't end up regretting this.'

'You won't,' Leigh promised her. 'Look, I'll have to take you round to introduce you to Mrs Johnson. You're her god-daughter and you're staying at the house to keep an eye for it while she's away.

'She's a nice old thing, although I don't think she quite approves of the idea of female private detectives.' Leigh pulled a wry face. 'She certainly isn't on her own there. She's only just moved into the house a month or so ago, so unfortunately she wasn't able to tell us very much about her neighbour. Only that he comes and goes rather a lot.'

'She's seen Ginny going into the house with him?'

Leigh sighed. 'Not as yet, thank God. I keep asking myself how I would feel if it was one of my two. What I'd do if, when they get to that age...'

'You've a long way to go before they do,' Debra pointed out to her. 'Sally is only eight and Bryony ten.'

'I know. Paul should have had them this weekend, but he cancelled at the last moment. I could have killed him, Debs . . . Not for my sake, but for theirs. Oh, Bryony put a brave face on it . . . said she expected that Daddy had a lot of work to do, and I went along with it. Work. Hah . . . more like some bimbo blonde occupying his time. Luckily Jeff came round, so we went into Chester, walked round the walls and then went on the river. He's so good with them, Debs. You can see in his eyes how much he'd have liked kids of his own. That must be so hard for a man, knowing that he can't be a father. That's why Alex divorced him, you know. Apparently, when they found out that his sperm count was too low for her to conceive, she told him that she couldn't stay married to him. That the reason she had married had been to have children.'

'He's a nice man,' Debra told her.

'A very nice man,' Leigh agreed.

Both of them started to laugh as Leigh mimicked one of the voices from a popular current TV advertisement. Although they were physically completely different, a sense of humour was something they shared.

Leigh had been ten when her father had married Debra's mother, and Debra had been four.

Leigh was like her father, tall, vigorous, with strong bones and thick curly brown hair.

Debra was like her mother, average height, slim, with delicate bones and the kind of honey-coloured hair that went strikingly fair in the summer.

Luckily, although it was very fine, it was also very thick. As an accountant, she often felt she would look more businesslike if she had it cut, but she had always worn it at shoulder-length, and she liked the versatility this gave her, plus the fact that her simple timeless style was easy to maintain.

Her mother and stepfather still lived in the same Cheshire village where she had been brought up. Leigh had bought a small house there after her divorce so that her daughters could be near to their grandparents.

Debra was now the proud owner of a very pretty little Georgian terraced house in Chester which was within walking distance of where she worked.

She was a happy, contented girl who enjoyed the friendships she shared with people of both sexes. At twenty-six, she was in no hurry to commit herself to a permanent relationship. A brief love-affair during the early years of her training when she had worked in London had taught her that the intensely passionate and deeply private part of her nature which she wanted to share with her lover was not always something that the male sex seemed to want. She had decided she wanted, needed a partner who would share her goals in life, who wanted security and calm; a family. Passion, she had decided, was not for her. One day she wanted to marry, but not yet. Leigh had once remarked that she was afraid of passion. She had, of course, denied it—too vehemently perhaps.

'Come on, I'll drive you over to Mrs Johnson's now,' Leigh told her.

She had arrived out of the blue at Debra's front door just over an hour earlier. Debra had been outside in her small back garden, watering the plants in her pots, and wondering if the current spell of good weather really merited the purchase of that wooden seat she had been coveting at the garden centre.

'Won't she mind, so early on a Sunday?' Debra protested, but Leigh shook her head, giving her a naughty smile as she told her,

'I've already warned her to expect us.'

Leigh had always been able to coax her into doing what she wanted, Debra admitted as she got into Leigh's car and secured the seatbelt.

Elsie Johnson's house was the next but last in a row of substantial Victorian houses in the suburbs of the city.

Leigh parked outside it with a flourish of gear-changing and sharp braking that made Debra wince a little.

All the houses in the row had short front gardens enclosed by a low communal wall, and from what Debra could see all of them were well maintained. It was the sort of quiet, respectable middle-class area that one would not normally have associated with the kind of situation Leigh had described to her, but if the man was as cold-blooded in his deliberate seductions as Leigh had implied then he probably found the area's respectability an asset.

'He won't be in now,' Leigh told Debra as she saw her glancing at the end house. 'He's taking Ginny out for the day. Her parents are afraid to refuse to let her see him in case she leaves home before they can help her to see just what kind of man he is.

'At seventeen, she's still barely more than a child still ... at least, she is compared with him, a man in his mid-thirties. I hate that kind of man.'

'Yes,' Debra agreed vehemently. 'So do I.'

She followed Leigh up to the front door.

Elsie Johnson had obviously seen them arrive because she opened the door before they could knock.

Half an hour later, as they drove away, Elsie having assured herself that it would be safe to leave her home in Debra's care, Leigh turned to Debra and thanked her.

'I suspect she thinks you're much more trustworthy than me. You always did have the gift of inspiring confidence in people.'

'Probably because they realise that, unlike you, I'm not going to do anything rash or reckless,' Debra told her with a smile.

Leigh laughed.

'I've got the tape and everything else you'll need in the boot. I'll give them to you when I drop you off. It will only be for a couple of days. I'll be back from London on Wednesday. I really am grateful to you, Debs. If we can get this contract to vet job applicants for Driberg's it will make all the difference to us.'

Debra pulled a face.

'I'm not sure if I approve of large companies using private agencies to vet potential employees.'

'I understand how you feel,' Leigh agreed. 'But it's a fact of commercial life these days, and if we don't get the commission then someone else will, and I have two growing daughters to support. Don't tell me that none of your clients has ever hinted that you might help them find a loophole in the tax laws,' Leigh added.

'We aren't that kind of firm,' Debra told her firmly. 'The advice we give our clients is always strictly within the terms of the law.'

Or at least it had been, Debra reflected later on when she was on her own and thinking over her conversation with her stepsister.

Would that continue to be the case now that the small old-fashioned firm she had worked for for the last three years had been amalgamated with a much more modern, thrusting Chester offshoot of a large multinational firm of accountants?

The multinational was putting in a new partner. None of them had met him yet, although they had all heard the rumours and whispers about how dynamic he was; about how determined he was to ensure that the new amalgamated firm would run efficiently and profitably. There had been no suggestion that jobs would go, but still there was an air of tension and uncertainty in the office, and Debra had been rather looking forward to her short break, especially since over the past few months she herself had been particularly busy, having had to take on the workload of a colleague who had left unexpectedly and not been replaced, in addition to working for her own clients.

She had planned to spend her time doing nothing more mentally demanding than working in her garden and redecorating her spare bedroom, but wryly she admitted that she could not really have refused to help Leigh out. Despite their differences, the two women were good friends, and Debra knew that in the same circumstances Leigh would have been the first to offer to help her.

The arrangement was that she would drive over to Elsie Johnson's in the morning just before Elsie was due to leave for her sister's, and that she would stay at the house until Leigh returned from London to relieve her on Wednesday.

If her stepsister's business continued to expand they would need to think of taking on extra staff, Debra mused as she packed. Both Leigh and her partner were adamant about preferring to take on only other women. They were not a tough, macho agency, Leigh had pointed out when Debra had gently reminded her that in doing so they could be accused of discrimination. The reason they were getting so many small commissions from other women was perhaps because it was a female-based agency and because, as women, they understood all too well how other members of their sex felt about male betrayal.

'Jeff helped out and he's a man,' Debra had pointed out.

'That was different,' Leigh had overruled her, adding that Jeff only helped them out as a favour. He didn't work for them.

In the morning Debra was careful to make sure that she arrived at Elsie Johnson's exactly on time.

As she had expected, she found the older woman was packed and waiting for her, a relieved expression touching her face as she opened the door to her.

Inside the house was shadowy and dark, the hall filled with old-fashioned Edwardian furniture.

Mrs Johnson was meticulous about security. Both outer doors had security chains as well as double locks; all the windows had locks as well, and Mrs Johnson herself reminded Debra of a timid little field-mouse, all nervously twitching whiskers and tensely anxious little body.

She would ring every evening, just to make sure that everything was all right, she told Debra before getting into her waiting taxi.

It was just as well that Leigh's clients were wealthy, Debra reflected later as she made herself a cup of coffee in the immaculately tidy kitchen. It was they who were paying Mrs Johnson for the use of her house, and paying her very generously as well.

Cautious and orderly by nature, Debra did not, as she suspected that Leigh would have done, find the immaculate tidiness of the house constricting.

She had brought all her own food supplies with her, and once she had had her coffee she unpacked her case in the small spare bedroom.

From upstairs she had a completely unrestricted view of the next-door house and rear garden, and if she left the landing window open she could, additionally, hear cars arriving at the front of the house.

Her instructions from Leigh were relatively simple. All she had to do was to monitor and then log down on the tape-recorder the details of anyone who visited the house.

Leigh had also provided her with a camera.

'Just in case we really get lucky and he brings one of his other women here,' Leigh had told her.

In any other circumstances Debra might have balked a little at such an intrusion of anyone's privacy, but she agreed with Leigh that a girl of seventeen, madly in love and totally obsessed with her lover, was in a dangerously vulnerable situation, and she could well understand Ginny's parents' concern for their daughter.

Before she had left, Elsie Johnson had told her nervously that there had been a good deal of commotion next door during the previous evening, raised voices, doors slamming, that kind of thing; but today all was peace and silence.

Debra had brought some work with her to help pass the time . . . not office work.

The previous summer she had accidentally become involved with a semi-private, semi-council-sponsored scheme which had involved individuals giving some of their spare time to young teenagers whom the council had in care.

It had been through a friend of a friend that Debra had originally heard of the organisation, and now she was a very committed member of the group, giving up a couple of evenings a month plus odd days at weekends to spend at the home.

The object of the exercise was to provide the teenager with someone with whom they could hopefully form a bond on a one-to-one basis, someone who, while not being their parents or having any authority over them, could help them with their problems in an adult way.

Debra was still in touch with the fourteen-year-old Amy, who was now back with her mother, and she was presently trying to form a bond with Karen, who had been taken into care having been abused by her stepfather, a withdrawn and obviously desperately unhappy girl. It made Debra's heart ache with compassion and sadness to see the look of despair and misery in her eyes.

If and when she ever managed to break through Karen's isolation, she hoped that she could do as she had done with Amy—take Karen out for small treats and help her to re-establish herself and to feel less institutionalised.

Now Debra was making a list of the problems she confronted in trying to make contact with Karen, and opposite these problems she was writing down the solutions she might find to them.

It wasn't easy; she found working with the teenagers emotionally and mentally draining, but the counselling and courses that all members of the group took had helped her to understand the children's problems and how best she could help them.

It was seven o'clock before she saw any sign of movement from next door.

She almost missed hearing the car pull up outside, and in fact she suspected that she would have done if she hadn't happened to be on her way downstairs at the time.

She frowned a little. The small compact Volvo was not somehow or other the kind of car she had expected the man to drive.

The net curtains hanging at the landing window obscured her vision of him and she had to flick them back a little as well as switching on the cassette which Leigh had impressed upon her she was to have with her at all times.

The man emerging from the car was tall and dark-haired. Before opening the garden gate he paused, glancing down the road, so that Debra had an unobscured view of his face.

A tiny shock of sensation curled through her, an immediate and disturbing physical response to him that made her check and tense.

He was frowning slightly and looked rather more formidable than she had imagined. He looked like a man used to being in control of himself and others. Warily Debra watched him. She had expected him to look different, less powerful, less compelling. She had assumed that he would have about him an air of weakness and self-indulgence, which this man most assuredly did not.

Before walking up the path he paused and then looked up at Elsie Johnson's house. Immediately Debra tensed. He *couldn't* possibly have seen her watching him, could he?

Her heartbeat suddenly accelerated, her muscles tensing. She dared not look out of the window in case he was still studying the house.

One minute went by and then another. This was ridiculous, she told herself crossly. There was no reason why she should not simply walk past the window, why she should feel so intimidated.

She took a deep breath and forced herself to move. Only when she was safely on the other side of the window did she allow herself a brief glance out of it. The man had gone inside the house.

Vigilantly Debra kept watch all evening, but all that happened was that she got cramp. All was quiet from next door. No one had arrived or left.

When she went to bed she set her alarm for six-thirty so that she could be on duty for seven when Jeff went home.

She didn't need the alarm. She hardly slept at all, and not just because she was in a strange bed, she admitted as she dressed. It wasn't just what she was doing that disturbed her; the man himself had unnerved her.

By seven o'clock she was eating her breakfast in front of the sitting-room window, where she had a clear view of the Volvo.

When by nine o'clock the Volvo was still there she began to panic a little.

Could he have left via the back door? Had he *guessed* that he was being watched? Had he perhaps even left during the night while Jeff was watching him?

At half-past nine she settled herself upstairs, where she had a clear view of the back garden and through the open landing window could hear any sound from outside at the front.

At eleven o'clock a taxi drew up alongside the Volvo and a woman got out. She was tall and elegant, expensively dressed, and as she paid off the driver Debra congratulated herself on noticing the wedding ring she wore.

Whoever she was, she certainly wasn't Ginny Towers, Debra reflected with satisfaction, and then she remembered that she was supposed to take photographs.

She had almost left it too late, and, as it was, she had to squash herself into the side of the window-frame and lean out of the window a little to get a good clear shot of the woman.

It was only as she withdrew that she realised that the man had opened the front door to welcome his visitor.

He had his back to her, and for some reason it gave her an odd sensation in her tummy to look down on him.

Vertigo, she told herself quickly, wondering if she dared risk trying to photograph them together without his noticing her, but it was too late. He was already ushering the woman inside.

Debra could hardly believe her luck when later on the two of them emerged into the garden. Despite her shaking hands, she managed to get several good shots of them standing talking together.

At three in the afternoon another taxi arrived and the woman left.

Standing beside the open landing window, Debra dutifully recorded this fact.

Although the man accompanied her to the taxi, he did not touch her in any way.

Leigh had described him as having a penchant for very young women. His visitor had not fallen into that field. She had been around his own age, early to mid-thirties.

Well, at least she had got some photographs of them together, Debra told herself as she went downstairs to make herself a drink.

She had just made it when the doorbell rang. She went to answer it without any sense of apprehension, her mind on the task Leigh had given her.

The safety chain wasn't on and she opened the door automatically without thinking, tensing in an alarm which came too late as she watched the man from next door march angrily into the hall and push the door closed behind him.

'Would you mind telling me exactly what you think you're doing?' he demanded curtly.

He was tall, Debra acknowledged, and strong as well, his body athletic and powerfully muscled. No doubt he found it paid to keep himself fit in order to impress his youthful victims. After all, a man of thirty-odd could not possibly hope to have the physical appeal of one much younger, she told herself, stubbornly ignoring the evidence of her own senses, which told her quite categorically that this man need not have any fear that younger rivals might present a more physically compelling appeal.

'I'm sorry,' she stammered as the guilty colour stormed her face. 'But I don't——'

'You don't what? You don't know what I'm talking about?' he interrupted her savagely. 'Like hell you don't. In someone old and alone, snooping on the neighbours can be understood and excused; in someone your age...well, let's just say you'd have to have some profound behavioural problems.'

As she heard the contempt in his voice Debra found that she wasn't shocked any more. She was angry...very, very angry.

'You're the one with the problems,' she told him unequivocally. 'Or don't you believe that it's a problem for a man of your age to want to seduce a girl barely over the legal age limit for sex? Men like you disgust me,' she added passionately. 'You deliberately lie and deceive. You don't care *who* you hurt...*how* many lives you destroy. It's just a game to you, isn't it? Girls like Ginny...too young and innocent to see what you really are.'

'Now just a minute,' he began grimly, but Debra had the bit between her teeth now and she wasn't going to stop. How *dared* he force his way in here and try to bully her...to accuse her, when he was the one...?

All her normal caution and restraint was swept aside in the passionate tide of feeling that engulfed her. She had been so lucky, so loved and protected as she had grown up, but she was well aware that not all young girls were, that there were men like this one ... like Karen's stepfather, who deliberately made young, vulnerable girls their victims; who destroyed them emotionally and ruined their lives. And *he* had the gall to stand there, glowering angrily at her.

'Why don't you simply leave her alone?' Debra swept on, ignoring his interruption. 'She's *seventeen* years old. Young enough to be your daughter.'

She saw him start and was grimly aware of the shock that momentarily darkened his eyes.

'I suppose you hadn't thought of it like that, had you? Men like you never do. You're too obsessed with your own appetites ... your own perversions.'

She heard the breath whistle out of his chest, and stopped, suddenly shocked by her own vehemence, suddenly realising her own vulnerability and danger.

'I don't understand what's going on here,' he told her, adding menacingly, 'but if you think I'm going to tolerate you spying on me, photographing me, *lying* about me, well, let me tell you, there are laws against the kind of thing you're doing.'

'There should be laws against people like you,' Debra spat shakily at him.

He was clever, she had to give him that, twisting things...accusing her...intimidating her with his alien male presence.

She was suddenly acutely conscious of the narrowness of the hall, of the closeness of his body, of the anger she could feel emanating from him.

'You won't be in any danger,' Leigh had told her. Suddenly she wasn't so sure.

'I want those photographs,' he told her flatly, 'and I want to know just what you think you're doing.'

'You *know* what I'm doing,' she told him. 'I'm trying to make sure that Ginny finds out exactly what kind of man you are...before it's too late.'

'Ginny?'

His deceit infuriated Debra. 'Yes. *Ginny,*' she snapped back at him. 'You know, the only-just-seventeen-year-old you're trying to seduce. You've been seen before, you know...bringing other girls here.'

As she threw a defiant look at him it seemed to Debra that something in his face suddenly changed, that there was some subtle alteration she couldn't quite define.

'You should be ashamed of yourself,' she hurled angrily at him. 'She's little more than a child. It's...it's perverted.'

He moved so quickly that she didn't have a chance to defend herself, taking hold of her, hauling her against his body, imprisoning her so completely that she actually found herself gripping hold of the front of his jacket to stop herself from losing her balance.

As she stared furiously up at him she could feel the frantic race of her own heartbeat. She could even, she recognised, feel the fiercely hard beat of his, just as she could feel the impact of his muscles against her own softness.

It was a disturbing sensation, and one that, to her shock, her body seemed to find distressingly sensual. Nausea rose inside her at the unacceptability of her physical response to him.

'That's the second time you've said that to me. The first was once too many. Whatever else I might be, I am not perverted,' she heard him saying grimly to her, 'and just to prove it...'

She had started to glance up at him as he spoke, an automatic reaction and one which he used to his own advantage, keeping her imprisoned between his body and the wall with one hand while the other held and cupped her face so that there was no way for her to avoid the alien masculine pressure of his mouth.

She could feel the anger in his kiss, the hard, fierce pressure that spoke of his antipathy towards her, but she could feel something else as well, a whisper of sensation, of awareness, curling like woodsmoke on a clear autumn day until it was everywhere. And as her body trembled she knew that he had felt it as well.

Later she told herself miserably that he at least had an excuse, as a man. It was in his genes to react with sexual aggression, but she had known none, and it wasn't even as though she didn't know exactly what he was.

But still her body responded to him, her muscles softening, relaxing, so that her body clung to him instead of rejecting him, and so that her mouth was pliant and eager beneath his, turning the kiss from what it had been to something very different indeed. Something *very* different.

And he responded to that difference, shifting his weight so that he was no longer imprisoning her but embracing her, the hand that cupped her face softening as his fingers slid into her hair, his mouth moving erotically on hers as his tongue-tip teased the moist softness of her lips.

Somewhere in the distance Debra could hear a sound, but it wasn't until he released her with a soft curse that she realised it was the telephone.

Abruptly she came back to reality, her face on fire with self-contempt, while unbelievably her body ached and yearned for the contact it had just lost.

'Aren't you going to answer it?' he questioned her as he reached for the door.

His anger had gone, a remote coolness taking its place, making her feel as though somehow she was the one who had transgressed.

Thoroughly flustered by the whole encounter, Debra stepped back from him. He was already opening the front door. She told herself that she was glad that he was going, that she was glad that the phone had started to ring when it did, but her body said rebelliously that it did not share those feelings.

It wasn't until he had actually closed the door behind himself that she realised that instead of answering the phone she had idiotically been standing watching him.

She turned round and hurried into the kitchen, lifting the receiver, her hand shaking.

'Yes, everything's fine,' she assured Elsie, trying to swallow the hard ball of disbelief and shock that was threatening to block her throat.

What on earth had got into her? she asked herself shakily ten minutes later. The whole incident had been so alien to the way she normally behaved.

She bit her lip, wincing as she remembered the way she had lost control of the situation. How *could* she have behaved so idiotically? Leigh would be furious with her, and no wonder.

And as for that accusation about his being a pervert... She stifled a moan of despair that rose in her throat.

Well, he couldn't have chosen a more devastating way of punishing her for it. Not in kissing her in anger. That she could have handled...*should* have handled with cold disdain and rejection instead of... She swallowed painfully, desperately trying to avoid remembering just how she had reacted to him, and then shivered a little as she tried to suppress the *frisson* of sensation that raced over her skin.

She wasn't normally like that. Didn't normally respond so immediately, nor so intensely, to being kissed. In fact, she couldn't remember a time when she had *ever* experienced that extraordinarily powerful surge of sensuality and desire.

Relentlessly she forced herself to keep watch throughout the evening, even though she knew that it was hardly likely that he would provide the evidence she needed, now that she had so idiotically given everything away.

She couldn't think what had come over her. Not only had she acted entirely against her own nature in losing her temper with him, not only had she let Leigh down, but she might also have ruined Ginny's parents' chances of making their daughter aware of the truth.

And on top of all that, as if it weren't enough, she had actually physically desired the man.

She gave a small shudder of self-contempt and despair.

CHAPTER TWO

'I'M SO sorry, Leigh. I just don't know what came over me. I've ruined everything.'

'No, you haven't,' Leigh assured her cheerfully as Debra reached the end of her explanation of what had happened.

'It seems that the owner of the house had served notice on our friend to leave. Apparently the rent hadn't been paid for several months and he had re-let the property and found another tenant. I suspect that the commotion Elsie overheard from next door the night before you moved in was our Mr Bryant, leaving under protest. The man you have been watching must be the new tenant, because Jeff told me that Bryant left in the early hours of the morning, and that he followed him as far as the motorway. Bryant was driving south and he was on his own.

'Ginny's mother has been in touch with me to tell me that she suspects he and Ginny must have had a row, because, although Ginny has been very weepy, she *has* told her mother that she isn't seeing him any more and that she doesn't want to. So, all's well that ends well.

'I'd have loved to see his face when you accused him of being a pervert,' Leigh grinned. 'Pity you didn't manage to capture *that* on film.'

Debra gave her an appalled stare.

'Do you mean that he wasn't...?'

'Bryant? It doesn't sound like it,' Leigh confirmed, 'and from your description he doesn't sound like it either. Your man seems to bear more resemblance to Superman than Mike Bryant,' she added with a touch of wry amusement.

Debra flushed, torn between relief that she hadn't messed everything up for her stepsister, and an appalled recognition of what she actually had done.

'You don't think he might report me to the police, do you?' she asked Leigh in a small voice.

'Saying what?' Leigh asked. 'That you took photographs of him and accused him of being a pervert? Hardly.' She grinned. 'Have you seen him again since he came round?'

Flushing again, Debra shook her head.

She had diligently kept a watch on him, monitoring his comings and goings, and while doing so she had been acutely aware of the way he would pause and look up at the house every time he left or entered next door, leaving her in no doubt that he was aware of what she was doing.

'Please don't ever ask me to help you out again, will you?' Debra pleaded feelingly as she handed Elsie's keys over to her stepsister.

Thank goodness she herself lived on the other side of the city and was unlikely to ever see *him* again. She gave a small shudder as she contemplated the embarrassment that *that* would cause her. And it made it worse, not better, hearing Leigh say that he had not been Mike Bryant. No wonder he had been so furious with her.

But who was the woman who had visited him and what was his relationship with her? Debra wondered as she drove home. Whoever she was and whatever her role in his life, it was no concern of hers, she told herself severely as she let herself into her house.

It felt blessedly familiar and safe, and as she closed the door behind her she told herself firmly that she was also closing the door on what had happened over the last few days. The best and most sensible thing she could do was, as Leigh had counselled her, to put it completely out of her mind.

She had not told Leigh everything, though, she acknowledged uncomfortably. She had not told her about that kiss.

Because it had nothing to do with helping Leigh out, she told herself swiftly. Nothing at all.

Was that the reason, or was it that she was still acutely aware of how quickly and immediately she had responded to him? She had shocked herself with that response and, even though she had tried desperately hard to forget it, to push it away from her and out of her mind, it was still there, threatening to haunt and punish her.

Not that she didn't deserve punishing, but not like this, not by waking abruptly in the night, aching and tense, knowing shamingly that she had been on the edge of reliving his kiss...that she had wanted to relive it.

What she ought to be punishing herself with was her own self-contempt, not some silly, immature yearning that belonged more properly to a teenager than an adult woman.

She spent the rest of the day diligently gardening and decorating, and on Thursday when she went to see Karen she admitted to herself that part of her outburst had probably been fuelled by her own emotional response to the trauma that Karen had endured. Not that he, even if he had been Mike Bryant, was guilty of the same sort of crime as Karen's stepfather, but Ginny's age and his maturity had sparked off all the anguish and helpless anger she had felt at Karen's plight.

Karen's social worker had already explained to her that Karen had been distraught at the thought of causing the break-up of her family and that her mother, far from supporting Karen, had accused her of trying to come between her and Karen's stepfather.

As she watched her now, withdrawn, silent and so obviously distressed, Debra's heart ached for her.

Very gently she started to talk to her, giving her time to respond, and then, when she did not, she simply continuing talking, keeping the tone of her voice as soothing and reassuring as possible, knowing that she must not try to rush things, or to pressurise Karen into lowering the barriers she obviously felt she needed to protect herself.

By Monday morning she had almost convinced herself that she had put the man and his kisses firmly to the back of her mind. On a very high shelf, lettered in red, 'Do not touch—danger', she told herself wryly as she walked to work.

Linda, the receptionist, smiled at her as she walked in, and asked her if she had had a good holiday.

'Not too bad,' Debra told her. 'I managed to weed the garden and to strip the paper off my spare bedroom. Anything interesting happened?'

She asked the question casually as she picked up her own post, not really expecting an affirmative answer, but, to her surprise, Linda nodded and then leaned conspiratorially over her desk.

'He's arrived. A fortnight ahead of schedule. Obviously wanting to catch us on the hop.'

When Debra looked puzzled, she explained, 'Him. You know, the partner from London who was due down next Monday—Marsh Graham.'

Debra's forehead cleared.

'Seems as if I've *really* missed out,' she commented with a smile.

She was not too concerned about Marsh Graham's appointment. She was a conscientious worker who knew she merited the praise she had received from her superiors. She was ambitious but not aggressively so, content to learn all that she could from her present position and to stay within it for another couple of years before embarking on something more challenging.

She felt she was too far down the hierarchy to be of much interest to the new man.

She was also very proud of the way she had streamlined her own systems, subtly and quietly adjusting the rather old-fashioned methods employed by her retired predecessor without stepping on anyone's toes. That she had found several rather disturbing errors and oversights was something else she had kept to herself, discreetly putting things right without drawing attention to them. After all, what genuine satisfaction was there in laying claim to a progress that was only made by correcting errors which should never have occurred?

'He's taken over old Mr Thompson's office,' Linda told her as though this were something totally unexpected, whereas to Debra it seemed perfectly acceptable that he should take over the empty office of the newly retired senior partner.

As she walked into her own office, calmly secure in her environment and her abilities, Debra felt a little of the tension and shock of the last few days ease from her. Here she felt in control of her life once again; here it was much much easier to push that kiss and its bestower safely out of her thoughts.

At eleven o'clock she received a telephone call from Marsh Graham's secretary, Mary, to say that Marsh wanted to see her.

'Nothing to worry about,' Mary told her cheerfully. 'He just wants to introduce himself to everyone and since you weren't here when he arrived...'

Firmly suppressing an impulse to ask Mary what he was like, Debra thanked her and replaced the receiver.

She was wearing a plain navy suit with a soft cream silk shirt, her tights were a toning blue-grey shade and her shoes the same navy as her suit.

It was a neat and very businesslike outfit, the sort of thing she always wore for work, apart from on those days when she had to visit one of her farmer clients, when she wore a fuller skirt and made sure she had her wellington boots in her car.

Even in summer, farmyards always seemed to be muddy and damp, and after ruining a pair of shoes she had sensibly made sure that she didn't ruin a second.

Her hair was caught back softly and neatly off her face with a navy silk scarf, and, having checked that her lipstick hadn't disappeared, Debra set off for Marsh Graham's office.

Mary smiled at her as she walked past her desk. 'Just go straight in,' she told her. 'He's expecting you.'

Debra did so, pushing open the door and then turning to close it behind her so that it wasn't until she turned round again that she actually properly saw the man standing up to greet her.

The blood seemed to leave the extremities of her body, her fingers, her toes and most dangerously of all her head, in a fierce, dizzying compression of shock as she stared at him in disbelief.

Impossible for her not to recognise him, or for him not to recognise her.

Even in her shock, her brain registered his momentary tension and the rapid dilation of his pupils, but he recovered faster than her, saying wryly, 'I take it that you *are* Debra Latham?'

Debra willed herself not to give in to the impulse to open the door and run.

'Yes,' she confirmed, her voice croaky and unsteady.

'It says in your file that you're employed here as a tax accountant.'

'Yes,' she agreed even more croakily.

Inadvertently she focused on him. The hands holding her file were long-fingered and strong, very male, the nails short and clean. A disturbing sensation quivered through her stomach as she remembered how he had touched her, sliding his fingers into her hair while he'd kissed her.

She made a small agonised sound in her throat, which immediately made him focus on her face.

'If you *are* a tax accountant, I wonder if you can explain to me exactly what it was you were doing last week? Or perhaps it's your hobby,' he added derisively. 'Spying on people.'

Debra could feel her face burning. One half of her wanted to tell him that how she chose to spend her free time had nothing whatsoever to do with him; the other reluctantly admitted that he had every right to demand an explanation. Had their positions been reversed, she would have wanted one.

But would she have got one? Would she have dared to challenge him the way he was challenging her?

If he had not held the position within the firm that he did she might have been tempted to ignore him, but morally he perhaps had a right to know what *had* happened, she admitted.

Haltingly she explained, unable to bring herself to look at him.

'Mistaking me for this man Bryant, I can understand . . . although I should have thought your stepsister would have supplied you with a photograph of him,' he said scathingly. 'Losing your temper and accusing him . . . or, rather, me of being a pervert . . .' He paused, and Debra discovered that she was holding her breath. It had been bad enough when she had turned round and recognised him, but to have to suffer this as well . . .

'Has it struck you,' he pursued grimly, 'just *what* danger you might have brought down on your own head, *had* I been this man Bryant, in making that kind of accusation? You were completely alone in that house, and, from your description of him, Bryant does not sound the type of man who would ignore that kind of accusation. It isn't one that any man would take lightly,' he added, watching her.

Unwisely Debra had lifted her head and turned to look at him, and now she was forced to withstand the full intensity of his thorough scrutiny of her flushed, defensive face.

He was lecturing her as though she were a child, she decided miserably, and it was obvious that he thought her completely irresponsible and incapable of calm, mature judgement. Her heart sank as she worried about how this might reflect on her in her career, and then acknowledged that he would have to be either a saint or inhuman not to let what had happened influence his assessment of her. In his shoes she doubted if she could have divorced herself from what had happened.

But if he *was* expecting her to apologise then he would just have to go on expecting.

She might have wrongly identified him, but *she* hadn't grabbed hold of *him* and physically punished him.

No, but she had responded to him; *had* turned that punishment into a few seconds of illuminatingly intense mutual intimacy. Because he had responded to her.

She realised that he had started talking again, only this time it was work he was discussing, saying something about wanting to look at some aspects of their tax planning service with her.

'Unfortunately I'm not going to have time until later in the week,' he added, dismissing her.

She had reached the door when he asked her coldly, 'What did you do with the photographs?'

Without turning round, she told him in a muffled voice, 'I burned the film without having it developed once Leigh told me that you weren't Mike Bryant.'

Why had he been so anxious about the film? she asked herself miserably as she half walked and half stumbled back to her own office. Or was it his companion he had wanted to protect, the married woman who had visited him?

A small shudder convulsed her body, a cold sweat breaking out on her skin despite the warmth of her office.

When she had comforted herself that she was hardly likely to see him again, fate must have been laughing out loud at her.

The incident had upset her enough as it was, without this extra burden of realising that she was going to have to work for him, without knowing that what had happened *must* influence his judgement of her, to her detriment.

And besides all that...

Besides all that, when she had incautiously looked across his office at him she had found herself focusing helplessly on his mouth, her body tensing with remembered pleasure and an unwanted frightening yearning to repeat it.

She got up, walking tensely over to her office window, and stared out. Please God, *not* that, she prayed desperately. Anything... anything at all, but *not* that.

She warned herself of the humiliation she would suffer if anyone, anyone at all other than herself, guessed what kind of effect he had on her, and *he* would be the first to lead the pack, she warned herself grimly.

She must not allow this ridiculous awareness of him to take root; she must destroy it, ignore it; it must not be allowed to flourish and to threaten the easy calmness of her life.

As she tried to concentrate on her work she wondered helplessly whether, had she not first met him in the way she had, had he not, as he had done, kissed her, but had they met for the first time today across his desk, she would have felt the same helpless surge of physical desire towards him.

Thankfully she didn't see anything of him for the rest of the day. She was just leaving at five-thirty when one of the other girls rushed into her office and apologised, 'I forgot to put it in your diary, but I made an appointment for you to go out and see Eric Smethurst tomorrow morning. Is that OK?'

'Yes,' Debra assured her.

Eric Smethurst was a fairly new client. A large, quietly spoken farmer who, her colleagues teased her, had something of a crush on her.

Debra had accepted their teasing good-naturedly. She half suspected they might have a point. Eric was thirty-two, hard-working, and very anxious to make a go of the run-down farm he had recently inherited from an uncle. He was also very shy and rather inarticulate, and, while Debra felt nothing for him in any remotely romantic sense, she did like him and wanted to do her best to help him to get the chaos his uncle had left behind him into proper order.

As she walked home she decided the only way to make sure that no one—but especially Marsh Graham himself—guessed about that vulnerable physical responsiveness she had to him was to treat him as coldly and distantly as she could. Not, she suspected, that she would be given the opportunity to do anything else.

Checking that she'd got her wellington boots in the boot of the car, Debra drove to work. The firm had its own private car park, and as she drove into it she immediately recognised Marsh Graham's Volvo.

Her mouth tightened a little as she deliberately looked away from it. She had overheard one of the secretaries chattering about Marsh to her friends the previous day, talking admiringly about the fact that he practised what he preached in that, when he said that he thought it wantonly selfish of greedy, self-important executives to demand larger and larger company cars, he obviously meant it, because he himself drove a small lead-free-fuelled car.

Privately Debra agreed with him. The days were gone when through ignorance one could allow oneself to believe that it wasn't up to each and every individual to be responsible and aware, not just on behalf of those closest to them, but on behalf of all humankind.

And, far from demeaning or lowering his stature in any way, the fact that he did not need to announce his success to the world by driving a large expensive car only seemed to reinforce the mental and emotional strength in him which Debra had recognised the first time she saw him.

She parked her car and got out, locking it before heading for the office.

'You're early this morning,' Linda commented as she saw her.

'I'm going out to see Eric Smethurst,' Debra told her. 'And I wanted to go through my post before I leave.'

'Eric Smethurst. Oh, the farmer. Isn't he the one who sent you those gorgeous flowers last Christmas?'

Debra knew she was flushing. She had her back to the corridor, but she was aware of the firm, male footsteps coming down it towards her.

A warning tingle ran down her spine and she knew without turning round that it was Marsh. She heard him stop behind her, felt in some subtle way the actual displacement of air caused by his presence.

'Are you sure it *is* just a business meeting?' Linda teased her.

Debra was acutely conscious of Marsh standing behind her. Even without turning round, she could sense his disapproval. Quickly picking up her post, she turned round, keeping her head down as she side-stepped him with a tense, 'Good morning,' before hurrying into the sanctuary of her own office.

The meeting with Eric went very much as she had expected. He wanted her advice about switching his accounting system on to a computer, something his uncle had scorned and refused to even consider, and Debra offered to arrange for the head of their own computer department to come out and see him.

'Margaux will have a much better idea than me of which system would be best for you,' she told him when he confessed that he had hoped *she* might be the one to advise him. Linda's light-hearted comment had alerted her to the danger of inadvertently encouraging him to believe theirs could be more than merely a business relationship. He was a very sensitive man, and the last thing she wanted to do was to hurt him, but she sensed from his reaction to her statement that he had picked up the subtle distancing message she was giving him.

It was almost one o'clock when she eventually left the farm. In addition to raising the subject of the computer and appropriate software package, Eric had also made tentative enquiries about how he might best set up a pension fund for himself, and Debra knew that once she got back to the office she would have a lot of work to do, liaising with her colleagues so that they could advise him.

Tax was her special field of operations, but Eric, like a good many of their smaller clients, preferred to deal with one specific person rather than each individual expert.

Debra had been wondering recently if there was some way in which this could be achieved, and so far she had not managed to come up with a solution, but she made a mental note to bring it up at the next office brainstorming session.

It was coming up to her stepfather's birthday, and she told herself that she must not forget to buy him a card. He was a keen gardener and she had ordered a very special old-fashioned climbing rose for him, which was presently being cosseted at her local garden centre.

As she drove back into Chester she glanced at her watch. She didn't really have time for lunch—she had too much to do—but if she drove home she could leave her car there and buy her stepfather's birthday card on her way back to the office.

Because she had been so young when her own father had died, and could not really remember him, she had formed a very close relationship with Don, her stepfather, and she smiled mischievously to herself as she picked out a card for him emblazoned with the words, 'To my most favourite man.'

She paid for it and tucked it between the two files she was carrying to make sure that it didn't bend.

Back in her office, she read quickly through her notes and then dictated an *aide-mémoire* for herself and a couple of memos, one to Margaux Livesey, the head of their computer department, and the other to Ian Rothsey, who was in charge of pensions and other allied insurance schemes.

She then rang through to Margaux's office to ask her if she could spare her half an hour.

'Just so long as it is half an hour, because I'm due to see Marsh after that. Come straight up,' Margaux offered.

Twenty minutes later, when Debra had finished outlining Eric Smethurst's situation, Margaux confirmed, 'I don't think we should have too much trouble sorting him out with a suitable package. It depends just how much he wants to take on board. There are farms which even have computer-controlled feeding systems for their livestock.'

'I don't think he'll want to go that far. Not at this stage. He can't afford to. When he inherited the farm from his uncle it was very run down. There were a lot of tax problems to sort out, back tax to pay, that sort of thing, and it's still very much touch and go whether or not he makes a success of it. I hope he does——'

There was a knock on Margaux's door.

'That will be Marsh,' she told Debra, standing up.

Debra stood up too, and as they walked to the door together Margaux opened it, smiling at Marsh and saying to Debra, 'Don't worry about your farmer. We'll make sure he gets the right package. You've obviously got a soft spot for him.'

Thanking her, Debra turned to leave, intending to step past Marsh, but he moved at the same time that she did, so that instead she virtually walked into him.

She had a heartbeat's space of time to control her expression, to avert her face and to lower her eyelids, while inwardly she was sickly conscious of the immensity of her body's ability to record and remember so many small and diverse details about him that she had immediately recognised his personal body scent, immediately recalled the exact configuration of muscles and sinews that were his, immediately sensed that the tension in his body was spiked with far more than any human being's automatic reaction to being walked into by another.

She was still shaking half an hour later, still unable to concentrate properly on what she was supposed to be doing, still so appalled and absorbed by the emotional shock of her physical response to him that when someone rapped on her office door she could barely manage to croak out a, 'Come in.'

She froze as the door opened and Marsh walked in, watching him warily as he walked over to her desk.

What *did* he want? Why had he come to see her? Her heart started to pound frantically.

'You weren't here last week when I explained to the others the way I consider that a business such as ours should be run,' he began, refusing the seat she offered him.

Since she was sitting down, while he stood, Debra immediately felt that he had put her at a deliberate disadvantage. She was tempted to stand

too, but she withstood the impulse, trying to
breathe deeply, to push away from herself her
awareness of him as a man and to concentrate
on the reality of him as her ultimate boss.

'I put a very high premium on professionalism, and as a part of that professionalism I do
not expect members of my staff to further their
private relationships in the firm's time. In fact,
I do not consider it wise for members of my staff
to form personal relationships with our clients at
all. And, if such a relationship *is* formed, I would
prefer it if the member of staff concerned asked
another colleague to take over the affairs of the
client. And in fact I find it extraordinary that I
should have to bring this matter up, especially in
view of the excellent, not to say glowing reports
in your staff records. "A valuable and hard-
working employee" was how they described you.'

For a moment Debra was too angry to speak.
How dared he think...suggest...? She could feel
the ire building up inside her, demanding an
outlet. She wasn't normally given to angry outbursts; they were foreign to her nature, but that
he should dare to suggest that she would behave
with such a lack of professionalism galled her to
the point where she could not contain what she
felt.

She stood up, angrily pushing back her chair,
facing him across her desk, flags of temper flying,
dark banners of colour against her pale skin, her
eyes bright with emotion.

'I do *not* use my work to facilitate my private relationships,' she told him furiously. 'I, like you, would consider that to be completely unprofessional and totally unacceptable.'

'Really?' His sarcasm stung. 'So tell me, how do you view using your holiday to do a spot of moonlighting, playing at detectives?'

So that was it, Debra recognised sickly. Perhaps she should have been expecting this kind of attack, but stupidly she had not, and because of that, she recognised, she had no real defences against it.

All she could think of to say was that what she did in her own private time was her own affair.

'Unless it happens to reflect on the standing of this firm,' he told her acidly, adding with scathing directness, 'What do you imagine might have happened had the victim of your mistake been a client or a potential client?'

Debra winced. She did not need him to ask her that question. She had asked it of herself often enough after Leigh had explained to her that she had been watching the wrong man.

'I've already explained what happened,' she told him shakily. 'It was a mistake...a misunderstanding.'

'In the same way, I assume, that it's also a *misunderstanding* that various members of the staff seem to think that your relationship with Eric Smethurst is based on a mutual interest in sex rather than on a mutual concern for his tax affairs,' he suggested grimly.

Debra gasped, outraged by what he had said.

'That's a ridiculous thing to say,' she told him.

'Is it? Why? Are you sure that your client does not have any sexual interest in you? How can you be sure? Has he told you so?'

Debra knew that hot guilty colour was scorching her skin, but there was nothing she could do about it.

'Of course he hasn't. It's hardly the sort of thing we would be likely to discuss,' she managed to say.

'One would hope not,' Marsh agreed quietly. 'But then, one would also hardly expect a client to send a dozen red roses as a Christmas present.'

'He grows them,' Debra told him stiffly. 'He's been trying to diversify... find other markets.'

'Well, since your relationship with him *is* only professional, you won't mind if I take over his account, will you?' he suggested dulcetly.

There was nothing Debra could say.

Furiously she watched in silence as Marsh left her office. She had worked hard on Eric's affairs, *very* hard, and she had just reached the stage where she felt she was actually making some headway, and now this.

Marsh Graham had no right to suggest that she was using her professional status to cloak a personal relationship with Eric. No right at all.

Now, when he had gone, she wished she had told him so; that she had been more forceful; but he had taken her so off guard.

When he had walked into her office she had somehow assumed that he had come to tell her that he had been aware of all that she had felt in that brief moment of impact in Margaux's office; that he had wanted to warn her that he was not remotely interested in her as a woman, even if he had kissed her.

To be virtually accused of using office time to further her personal relationship with Eric Smethurst had stunned her so much that she still felt as though she was in shock.

And to have the account taken from her... That had been both underhand and unfair.

And unnecessary?

Of course it was unnecessary, she told herself, but her conscience wouldn't let her ignore how surprised and disturbed she had been to receive those roses, and how she had felt even today when she was with Eric, how aware she had been that, with the least encouragement from her, he would want to take their relationship on to a far more personal level.

If he had approached her in a different manner, if he had suggested that it was as much for her sake as the firm's that he take over the account, wouldn't she have found that her disappointment at losing Eric's business just when she was beginning to experience the professional satisfaction of having got his affairs in order was tempered by the knowledge that she was beginning to worry just a little about Eric's feelings towards her?

But Marsh *hadn't* behaved as a compassionate, considerate superior. He had belittled her, and acted with such breathtaking highhandedness that even now she could hardly believe it had actually happened.

CHAPTER THREE

DEBRA glanced at her watch. She was going to have to hurry if she was going to make tonight's meeting on time. She had only half an hour in which to get ready and to drive across Chester to Brian Hughes's house.

Brian Hughes was the local co-ordinator for Debra's voluntary group. Once a month they all met at his house to discuss with one another their progress and problems.

Debra was particularly anxious to attend tonight's meeting. She felt she was not making any progress at all with Karen, and she was worried that she might be hindering the girl rather than helping her. She wanted to discuss this with Brian and to ask the group's advice.

As she changed into her jeans and a sweat-shirt she firmly pushed the day's events out of her mind. It wasn't fair to Karen or to the others in the group to allow her own problems and emotions to intrude when she should be concentrating exclusively on them.

Her brain, her emotions were still quivering with the resentment and anger she had felt during her interview with Marsh, and worriedly she admitted that, behind the anger she had every right to feel, there was also a disturbing element of pain and hurt at having been misjudged by him; the kind of pain and hurt that came from being emotionally vulnerable to the person giving the criticism.

She did not want to dwell on that particular aspect of her reaction. It was too dangerous.

She was just in time for the meeting and the last to arrive, or so she thought until Brian welcomed her and then added, 'A new member will be joining us tonight. He's been part of a similar group working in London and he has been given our group as a contact by them.

'I suspect we'll find he has a very worthwhile input to make, since his group specialise in dealing with the more aggressive element of youngsters taken into care.'

For once, *she* had the advantage of surprise, Debra reflected ten minutes later when Marsh arrived and Brian started to introduce him.

She saw the look he quickly masked as he saw her and was grimly surprised that now it was his turn to be caught off guard. She had suspected from the way Brian had described him that their new member might be Marsh, but he soon overcame his surprise, telling Brian, 'Debra and I already know one another. In fact, we work together.'

Someone made room for Marsh to sit down next to Debra on the sofa, and Debra hoped that Marsh wasn't aware of the way she surreptitiously edged herself away from him, something it was difficult to do when his weight meant that her body inclined naturally towards him.

Like her, he was dressed casually in jeans and a sweat-shirt, the unisex uniform that somehow was not in the least unisexing on him.

Perhaps it was the breadth of his shoulders beneath the soft sweat-shirt, or maybe it was the hard-muscled tautness of the thigh resting against her own.

Whatever it was, Debra wished that he were not sitting next to her. She was so acutely conscious of him that she could barely concentrate on what everyone was saying, and she almost didn't hear Brian when he asked her, 'How are you getting on with Karen, Debra?'

Before she could reply he turned to Marsh and explained, 'Karen was a victim of sexual abuse by her stepfather. Her mother has rejected her, blaming her for what happened. Karen is extremely withdrawn and undergoing specialised counselling.

'Debra has a very gentle touch, and we've been hoping that she might be able to form a bond with Karen.'

Debra felt the sofa depress as Marsh turned to look at her. He was studying her gravely, the grey eyes thoughtful and observant.

She was intensely aware of the warmth of his thigh against her own. She tried to shift her weight to escape it, wriggling tentatively away from him and then stopping, tensing as she saw the way his eyes suddenly darkened, his pupils dilating. Instantly she was transported back to the hallway of Elsie's house, her body pressed up against his while Marsh kissed her and she clung to him, her mouth opening, her body pleading.

Heat washed over her. Her mouth had suddenly gone dry and her muscles ached with tension. Somehow she managed to drag her gaze away from him.

'I . . . I just don't seem to be making any progress at all,' she told Brian huskily, trying to dismiss what she was feeling and to concentrate instead on her awareness that she just wasn't managing to make any contact with Karen.

'I feel she's evading me. Evaluating me,' she continued, groping for the right words to explain her sense of failure. 'I want to help her, but . . . she looks at me sometimes as though *I'm* the child and she's the adult, and when I think of what she's been through I feel so helpless . . . I feel as though my being there at all is almost an insult to her . . . betrays a prurient curiosity about her, and I think that's what she feels as well.'

'I think it's more likely that she's just testing you.'

The sound of Marsh's voice, controlled, evaluating, made Debra turn her head to focus on him.

He was looking directly at her, and to her shock she realised that there was no criticism, no anger in his eyes, just a very real awareness of her fear that she was not the best person to help Karen.

Her heart started to beat far too fast, and she had to suppress the urge to start breathing more quickly and shallowly.

'I think you should persevere,' Marsh continued, but now he was speaking not just to her but to everyone else as well as he added, 'We've had similar experiences with our group, situations where we've felt that we just aren't being of any benefit at all, and it's only later that we've realised that their silence and apparent rejection was simply a way of testing us... of wanting to be assured that we really do care.'

There was a small silence while everyone assimilated what he had said, and then Brian said thoughtfully, 'I think Marsh could be right, Debra.'

One of the others had started to talk about the problems he was having with one of the boys at the same home as Karen. Debra knew him by sight and frowned as she listened to Gary Evans explaining that he was concerned about the boy's uncontrolled outbursts of violence.

'He bullies the others. We know that, and he's capable of extremely violent, even vicious behaviour, but in mitigation we have to take into account the fact that he's been beaten brutally by his father almost all his life. Violence is the only thing he knows.'

'Have you thought about getting him on one of these outward-bound-style courses? We found we got very good results from them,' Marsh suggested helpfully.

The meeting went on rather longer than usual, breaking up just after eleven o'clock, and, as luck would have it, probably because they were the last to arrive, once they were outside Debra discovered that her and Marsh's cars were parked behind one another, slightly further down the road than the others.

It was impossible for her to avoid walking towards her car with him. Nervousness made her make some tritely foolish comment about the coincidence of running into him at the meeting.

He had stopped walking and she was obliged to stop as well. They were out of earshot of the others and no one could overhear them as he bent his head and said quietly, 'I feel I owe you an apology for this afternoon.'

Instinctively Debra turned away from him. Her heartbeat had increased again and was far too rapid. Much more of this and she would probably start hyperventilating, she told herself irritably.

'As I said at the time, my relationship with Eric is purely a business one,' she told him huskily.

'Yes. I'm sorry. It's just that a rather unfortunate situation developed in our London office, culminating in the wife of one of our clients storming in and accusing the member of staff involved of trying to steal her husband and even threatening to sue. I don't know how, but one of the tabloids got hold of the story and, while there was no real truth in what they printed, it did put the firm in a very embarrassing position.

'It was that that made me over-react this afternoon. I realise that the comments I over-heard were simply made to tease. In fact, Margaux informs me that you of all people are the last person who would become personally involved with a client.'

He had *discussed* her with Margaux. Her distaste must have shown in her eyes, because he added quietly, 'I told her that I was taking over the account. She asked me why. When I explained my concern she immediately told me that I was worrying unnecessarily.'

'*I* told you that I wasn't involved with Eric,' Debra couldn't resist pointing out.

'Yes,' he agreed. 'But you didn't say that he was equally uninvolved with you. In my experience a man does not send a woman red roses simply to show her that he can grow them.'

Debra bit her lip.

'I have been a bit concerned that he might...that he could be thinking... I'd already made it clear to him though that I couldn't...that I wasn't...'

'That what? That you didn't want him?'

He was, Debra realised, standing much closer to her. She could hear car doors slam and engines start as the others left. She could feel the cool evening breeze stirring her hair; she could feel the silence and the tension. She could feel her own overwhelming need to take that one step forward which would bring her so intimately close to him that her body would actually be touching Marsh's. Out of the corner of her eye she saw his hand lift. A quiver of sharp sensation pierced through her as she remembered how she had felt to have his hand touching her face, his palm warm against her skin, his fingers stroking into her hair, the pads firm against her scalp, his thumb touching the corner of her mouth, his breath warm against her lips before he touched them with his tongue.

Somewhere further down the road a car backfired. Debra shuddered quickly, stepping back from him, thankful that it was dark and that he couldn't see how flushed she was, how aroused her body. Thank goodness for the thickness of her sweat-shirt, disguising the tautness of her nipples as they pushed against her clothes.

Quickly she turned towards her own car, distancing herself from Marsh and the danger he represented. She heard him take a step as though he meant to follow her and then stop.

His goodnight was brief, curt almost.

Shakily Debra let herself into her car.

It had been the most extraordinary evening, and the most extraordinary part of all had been Marsh's apologising to her. That was something she had not expected. Would he have done so, though, if Margaux hadn't unwittingly substantiated her own statement that she was not personally involved with Eric Smethurst?

'You haven't forgotten that it's Don's birthday this weekend, have you?'

Debra smiled into the receiver. 'No, Mum, I haven't forgotten.'

Don's card was in front of her on her desk. She had put it there this morning to remind her to write and post it.

She was due to visit Karen this evening. She still felt she wasn't making any progress. Karen was still withdrawn from her. Was Marsh right? Was Karen testing her?

Marsh!

It was now two days since he had apologised to her, and since then his whole attitude to her had been different...warmer, gentler, more open.

She must not read something into that which did not exist, she warned herself. She had heard on the grapevine that he wasn't involved with anyone and that his last serious relationship had ended while he was working in the States.

So there was no other woman in his life. That did not mean that...

That what? That there was a place for her? She knew that...of course she did. And besides, she would have to be an idiot to think that just because he had apologised to her, just because he was being pleasant to her, it meant anything more than that he was simply being pleasant to a colleague.

Even so... Rather like a child opening a forbidden drawer, she closed her eyes, remembering how she had felt when he kissed her, savouring each second of that memory, sharply aware of the *frissons* of sensation that it set off within her body.

That he had initially kissed her in anger, she chose not to allow into her memories. It was that other later kiss she recalled. Her eyes still closed, she leaned back in the chair, her body responding to the sensual messages of her thoughts. She squirmed voluptuously as she conjured up the physical sensation of Marsh's body against her own.

'Debra, are you all right?'

She shot upright, her eyes opening, her face hot, to find Marsh himself standing on the other side of her desk, watching her, a thoughtful expression in his eyes.

He couldn't *possibly* know what she had been thinking, she assured herself, feeling thoroughly flustered and guilty as she fibbed that she had just been thinking about one of her cases.

Marsh was frowning, she discovered when she ventured a brief look at him. His head was turned away from her and he was looking down at her desk, at the birthday card she had bought Don.

'It's for my stepfather,' she told him, half gabbling the words. 'It's his birthday this weekend. I put it there so I wouldn't forget to post it.'

'Your stepfather.' Unexpectedly he smiled at her.

'Yes, it's a joke between us that he's always been my favourite man.'

'Always?' The question was lightly delivered, but for some reason it made her flush. 'Hasn't there been *anyone* in your life who's tempted you to change your mind?'

Debra gulped, her thoughts chaotic. In another man she might almost have suspected that the question cloaked a personal interest in her answer, but she hastily suppressed such a thought and answered lightly, 'Not so far.'

'Do your parents live locally?'

The mundanity of the question relaxed her taut muscles slightly.

'Sort of. They live in Tarford. It's about twenty miles away. Leigh, my stepsister, lives there as well. She moved there after her divorce. She wanted the girls to be close to their grandparents.'

'Leigh?' Marsh questioned, and then nodded. 'Ah, yes. The detective agency. An unusual career for a woman.'

'Leigh and her partner felt there was a need...that other women would find it easier to consult a woman,' Debra told him slightly defensively.

'I wasn't criticising,' Marsh told her mildly. 'I was just curious. And it was your stepsister you were standing in for when you and I——'

'Yes,' Debra interrupted him quickly. She still felt so uncomfortable about what had happened.

'I suppose you must have thought when Lynn arrived with those papers for me that she and I...' He stopped, and then told her wryly, 'She works at the London office and she was bringing me some documents I needed.'

'I'm sorry,' Debra told him unhappily, and then added impulsively, 'I wish the whole thing had never happened.'

'Do you?'

The way he said it made her swing round. He was looking directly at her, his attention focused on her mouth.

Her pulse-rate ricocheted. She was gripped by a thrill of sharp sensation, a mixture of exhilaration and disbelief that shocked her body as intensely as though she had received a sudden burst of adrenalin.

Helplessly she looked back at him, knowing that her pupils were dilating, that her mouth was softening, her lips parting; knowing that he must be as aware as she was herself of all the small sensual signals her body was giving him, but either unable or unwilling to do anything to conceal them.

'I don't,' he told her softly. 'Not *all* of it.' He paused, and then continued, 'Look, there are a couple of points about Eric Smethurst's affairs I wanted to go over with you. I was wondering if we could have a drink after work. I'd suggest dinner, but I'm seeing a client later.'

Almost choking on her disappointment, Debra shook her head.

'I'm sorry, I can't,' she told him. 'Not tonight.'

She held her breath, praying that he would suggest another evening, but to her disappointment he merely said calmly, 'Never mind.'

For far too long after he had gone Debra sat staring tensely into space.

Had she completely misread the situation? *Had* he been deliberately flirting with her, or had she simply imagined it? *Had* he been referring to the kiss they had shared when he said that he did not want to forget 'all of it', or had that simply been wishful thinking on her part?

And when he had suggested they discussed Eric's tax problems after work over a drink, *had* it been because he wanted to spend time with her, or had it simply been an ordinary, mundane way of extending office hours? After all, it was hardly unusual for two colleagues to meet to discuss work over a drink.

But if he had wanted to see her for more personal reasons, was that what *she* wanted?

Physically she felt a compulsion towards him, a desire...a need she could neither explain nor ignore. But did she actually want him to recognise that desire or to reciprocate it?

She moved uneasily in her chair. One day she hoped that she would meet someone…a man for whom she felt the kind of deep, steady, mature love which she felt was essential for the kind of relationship she wanted; a relationship founded on mutual respect and liking, on shared interests and humour; on shared goals; but she had never envisaged a place in that relationship for the kind of high-voltage and far too intense sexual clamouring of her body and senses that she experienced when she was with Marsh.

That kind of high-risk physically based relationship was the last thing she wanted in her life. She had witnessed its effects on others, seen how all-consuming it could be, how potentially destructive, exhausting the emotions of its victims, burning them out until there was nothing left.

Leigh and Paul had had that kind of relationship. Leigh had never made any secret of the fact that sex was the prime motivating force between them. She had even, she had once told Debra, gone on wanting Paul sexually long, long after she had known that their relationship had nothing left in it of love.

'I don't love him,' she had said. 'But, God help me, I still want him,' and Debra had heard the self-loathing in her voice and had shivered a little at the sound of it, promising herself that she would never fall into the same trap.

And she hadn't done. Until now!

If she gave in to her desire for Marsh, if she encouraged it and he reciprocated, what would happen?

She gave a small shudder of apprehension. They might be lovers, but would they *love*, and if they did would it be a love that would endure...would she want it to endure? Wouldn't she be safer, wiser, keeping to the path she had already mapped out for herself, establishing herself securely in her career and then thinking cautiously and sensibly about marriage and a family... finding someone who shared her ideals and her beliefs...someone who would be her friend and partner first, someone who, like her, would put the needs of their children above those of his own senses, his own body?

Highly sensual, highly sexual men were notoriously weak when it came to ignoring temptation. Good for a fling, but not for anything else, as Leigh had once said bitterly of Paul.

She had no evidence to suggest that Marsh was promiscuous—rather the opposite—but he was certainly not the safe, tame, low-sexed partner she had envisaged for herself, and, if she allowed herself to get involved with him, ultimately he would hurt her, or rather she would hurt herself through her own inability to control the intensity he aroused in her.

She didn't want that intensity. It was a part of herself she rejected.

She remembered as a child her mother sigh and say softly, 'Poor Leigh. She suffers so much when she loves because she's so intense.'

Leigh had gone through a series of intense and volatile emotional relationships during her teenage years, and Debra had watched and sworn that she would not suffer as Leigh had done.

She resented her responsiveness to Marsh, she admitted, and she was obsessed by it, at the same time unable to resist reliving over and over again how she had felt when he kissed her. Her very compulsiveness frightened her, and yet she knew that if she had not been seeing Karen tonight she would have gone out with him.

She was glad that she had the weekend ahead of her to give her time to put things into perspective, to help her to clear her mind and to concentrate on reality rather than fantasy.

'Hello, Karen. How are you?'

Debra smiled warmly, pretending not to notice Karen's averted face and tense body.

'Can we go out?'

The curt question startled her, but Debra quickly covered her shock. Karen had never actually addressed any comment directly to her before, and she had certainly never asked her anything like this.

Cautiously warning herself not to read too much into this breakthrough, Debra nodded and said as casually as she could, 'Yes, I should think so. Where did you have in mind?'

The thin shoulders shrugged. 'Doesn't matter...anywhere. I just want to get out of here.'

Debra felt a small *frisson* of anxiety. Karen looked thinner than when she had last seen her. She had very pretty curly hair, which she normally kept scrupulously clean, but today it looked lank and dull.

Karen's social worker had told Debra that Karen had once had very long hair but that she herself had cut it off.

'She had literally hacked it off in chunks. That was what first alerted her form teacher to what might be going on. Victims of incest, particularly once they reach their teens and become more aware, often try to mutilate themselves in some way, partially out of self-punishment and partially to deter their abuser.'

'How about McDonald's?' she suggested, thinking quickly. 'I've got my car. We can drive into Chester.'

She held her breath, only releasing it when Karen nodded.

She had to obtain permission to take Karen out, of course, but it was readily given. Karen was not, as some of the children were, an absconder.

She sat silently in the car as Debra drove into the city and parked.

It was a pleasant evening, the sun still out, the city busy with locals and tourists alike.

Karen was wearing a pair of jeans that seemed too big for her and an oversized sweater, not an unusual outfit for a girl of her age, but Debra knew that Karen had a stronger motive than most for concealing, if not rejecting, her sexuality, and she saw the disparaging, bitter looks the girl gave a small group of her peers dressed in mini-skirts, standing chattering outside one of the shops.

'Tarts,' she muttered under her breath as they walked past them.

Debra knew better than to chastise her. It was no wonder that Karen felt resentful of them, resentful of their ability to enjoy their growing up, their womanliness...a right which had been ruthlessly taken from her.

McDonald's wasn't over-full. They had arrived during the lull between the early- and late-evening business. They collected their food, Debra trying not to wince at the sticky milkshake Karen ordered to go with her burger.

She would never understand the appeal of such food, but she could not deny that it did have an appeal. Her two nieces loved it, despite Leigh's complaints that it was loaded with sugar.

Karen ate her food in silence. She was sitting facing the window. Suddenly she tensed, the blood leaving her face.

'It's him,' she told Debra in panic. 'He's followed me. He's coming in.'

Shocked, Debra turned her head, thinking that Karen must have seen her stepfather, but all she could see was a sullen-looking teenage boy.

'Karen,' she said gently, 'it's all right.'

'No, it isn't,' Karen told her.

She was shaking, and Debra could see panic in her eyes. Karen stood up, pushing her chair away from her, her milkshake carton falling on the floor as she stumbled into the table.

Debra stood up as well, terrified that she might lose her as Karen rushed out into the street.

The boy, Debra noticed, was watching them, a knowing and somehow rather intimidating look in his eyes.

As she hurried past him, intent on catching up with Karen, she heard him say tauntingly, 'Great tits.'

She stiffened instinctively, stunned not so much by his comment, but by his self-assurance. He couldn't be more than fourteen or fifteen at the most, but, despite that, there had been something in the way he looked at her that told her that he wasn't simply repeating parrot-fashion a comment he had heard made by someone older.

She caught up with Karen just as the girl was about to dart across the road in front of an on-coming car.

Grabbing hold of her, Debra hauled her back. Tears were pouring down Karen's face. She was shaking . . . not trembling, but shaking.

Instinctively Debra wrapped her arms around her, holding her as tightly as she could, rocking her as she held her, not knowing what had happened, just knowing that she needed her comfort, her help.

When she felt she was calm enough she walked her back to the car, but then, instead of taking her back to the home, she took her to her own house.

Once they were inside she poured Karen a glass of milk and made herself a cup of coffee.

'What is it? What's wrong, Karen?' she asked gently.

It was like floodgates opening, forced apart by the weight of emotion and despair behind them.

It was him, the boy, Karen told her. He had started following her round, saying things to her, calling her names. He called her a slag, and said that she was a prostitute. He had followed her into her room one afternoon. He had had a knife. He had told her that he would use it on her if she didn't do everything he told her.

Someone had come in and he had gone away, but she was frightened of him, Karen told her. Frightened of the way he kept looking at her.

Debra didn't make the mistake of disbelieving her. Even if she hadn't been able to hear the loathing and terror in her voice, what she had seen in the boy's eyes, despite his youth, confirmed everything that Karen was saying to her.

'I'll have to tell the superintendent, you know that, don't you?' she told Karen gently. 'Not just because of you, Karen. Think...if he's threatening you he could be threatening other girls as well.'

'If he finds out I've told you...'

'He won't,' Debra assured her.

The superintendent heard her out in silence when she asked to speak to him alone and told him what had happened.

'I was afraid of something like this happening. He's got a record of bullying and worse. He shouldn't really be here—or rather children like Karen shouldn't be here. And we call it taking them into care.

'Don't worry. I'll make sure that Karen is properly protected.'

'And the boy?'

'Another member of your group has been trying to help him to no avail. I understood you've got a new member, Marsh Graham. Apparently he's going to take over. It seems he's had some experience in this field. He's suggesting a course where the boy can find a legitimate vent for some of his frustration and aggression.

'Personally I think it might be too little too late. Thank God Karen confided in you.'

It wasn't just Karen who was afraid of the boy, Debra admitted later as she washed up her supper things. She too had experienced unease and apprehension when he looked at her.

Fourteen. She hoped Marsh *could* help him, otherwise who knew what type of man he might grow up to be?

CHAPTER FOUR

DEBRA had a meeting first thing in the morning. It was an innovation Marsh had instituted, an opportunity for everyone to get together and to discuss work problems.

Normally Debra would have joined in the discussions enthusiastically, but she couldn't put Karen out of her mind.

She had phoned the home before leaving for work.

Karen was fine, the superintendent had assured her. She was not to worry. But she was worrying. She couldn't help it.

She was still thinking about Karen when the meeting broke up. She got up to leave the office with the others, but Marsh stopped her.

'If you've got a minute, Debra.'

She waited apprehensively as the others left, aware of their curiosity about why she had been asked to stay behind.

She could feel the anxiety mounting inside her. Had she done something wrong? Something she herself knew nothing about? Marsh had Eric Smethurst's file; had he found some error in it, something she had overlooked or neglected?

An uncomfortable panicky feeling tightened her chest. Marsh opened the door from the conference-room to his own office.

Nervously Debra preceded him inside.

'Sit down, Debra,' Marsh invited her. 'Would you like some coffee?'

She shook her head, her stomach churning too tensely.

'You seemed rather preoccupied this morning,' Marsh commented as he sat down opposite her.

His desk was between them, a heavy, solid and definitely inanimate block of wood, but it still didn't prevent her from being acutely aware of him.

She could smell the clean freshness of his soap, and her heart somersaulted at the recognition; at the subtle invasive memory of that same smell on his body when he had held her in his arms.

She pulled back quickly from the thought. She had promised herself that she was going to be sensible; that she must concentrate on the plans she had made for herself. She was afraid of the desire Marsh aroused within her, she acknowledged, but that fear was her route to safety.

'I know it isn't always easy, adjusting to changes in our working lives,' Marsh continued. 'And the more sensitive we are, the more we react to those changes.

'I admit I had my doubts about taking over down here. It's always difficult when two firms amalgamate. There's bound to be confusion and a certain amount of resentment. People coming in can sometimes seem to be insensitive, even unfair.'

Debra frowned. Was he suggesting that he might have been unfair towards her?

'It's true that I *am* only human,' Marsh continued. 'But I would hate anyone to think that I would allow my personal judgements and...' He paused and frowned, getting up and walking over to the window, his abruptness startling Debra. There was a tense set to his shoulders as he stared out of the window. 'And my feelings,' he went on tersely, 'to influence my professional judgement. You've handled Eric Smethurst's affairs very well. I didn't take over the case because I doubted your ability to deal with it, Debra. Perhaps I did act too precipitately but...'

He thought her silence this morning had been caused by the fact that he had taken over Eric's affairs, Debra recognised, and now he was trying to reassure her that that was not the case.

Immediately she corrected him.

'It isn't *that*. I do understand why you felt that someone else should handle Eric's business. It...it isn't work at all,' she admitted a little guiltily, hardly surprised to see the way he was frowning when he turned round to focus on her.

'I'm sorry. I know I shouldn't bring my personal problems into work with me, but I saw Karen last night. She was very distressed. One of the boys in the home has been threatening her.'

Debra gave a small shiver, her eyes suddenly bleak and just a little afraid.

'I saw him myself. We were in McDonald's. He was very...intimidating. I've had a word with the superintendent at the home. He promised that he'd do something.'

'This boy,' Marsh questioned her tersely, 'did he threaten *you*?'

Debra stared at him, caught off guard by his perception.

'No...not exactly. But there was something about the way he looked at me...a...a knowingness...a...' She shook her head. 'I can't describe it, but I knew somehow that Karen had every reason to be afraid of him.

'I shouldn't be telling you this.'

'Rubbish—of course you should. That's one of the reasons I'm here; to listen to everyone's problems.'

'*Work* problems,' Debra told him wryly, 'not personal ones, but that wasn't what I meant. This boy...' She took a deep breath. 'It's the one we were talking about at the meeting, the one you'll be dealing with.'

She bit her lip, hanging her head a little. The aims of their group were to help each and every child they had contact with, no matter what they might have done, and she felt it was wrong of her to tell Marsh something that might prejudice him against the boy, no matter how justified she knew her feelings and fears to be.

'I see.' Marsh turned back to the window. 'So it was Karen you were seeing last night when you couldn't meet me after work for a drink?'

He swung round as he asked the question, catching Debra off guard. She stared at him.

'Yes. Yes...that's right,' she confirmed, a little confused.

His smile was unexpectedly relaxed and warm.

Debra blinked and tried to fight off the slow, sweet, toe-curling sensation that poured over her. She felt slightly dizzy, she recognised, and, although outside it was a rather dull grey day, she felt as though the sun had suddenly burst through the cloud and was shining with dazzling intensity. Her heartbeat quickened, a thrill of fierce joy and happiness bubbling up inside her.

And all because one man had smiled.

'I know we got off on the wrong foot,' Marsh was saying softly to her now. 'But that's behind us now. We have a lot in common, you and I, Debra.'

Debra fought valiantly not to respond to the warm promise of his voice.

He was probably just at a bit of a loose end, she warned herself. He was, after all, new to the area, and couldn't know many people yet. No doubt he missed the hectic social life he had probably enjoyed in London.

To cover what she was feeling she said quickly and a little shakily, 'Well, we are both accountants.'

She could see the laughter in his eyes.

'Yes, we are, but that wasn't quite what I meant. I was thinking more in terms of our...personal compatibility than the fact that we happen to have chosen the same career.'

Their *personal* compatibility. Debra swallowed, her thoughts rioting chaotically.

'So you're going home to...Tarford, wasn't it...this weekend?' Marsh continued easily. 'Try not to worry too much about Karen. I can understand your concern, but now that the home is aware of the situation I'm sure they'll keep an eye on it.'

Nodding, Debra stood up.

If it had not been for the fact that she felt so uneasy about her physical awareness of Marsh she would have been walking back to her office on air, full of admiration for his compassion and understanding, she admitted as she left him.

As it was, she was filled with a frenetic combination of elation and anxiety that made it impossible for her to sit still and work.

Had he *really* said what she had *thought* he'd said, and what was she going to do about it if he had meant it?

Cravenly she acknowledged that, like the ostrich with its head in the sand, she would do nothing unless he did.

She might, after all, have misunderstood him. He might simply have been intimating that they could develop a platonic friendship based on their mutual involvement with the children's group, and no more than that.

It was unnecessary for her to go looking for imagined problems, she reminded herself wryly. She already had enough very real ones to contend with.

'Debra, the rose is perfect.'

Debra smiled her happiness at her stepfather's pleasure in her gift as he leaned over and kissed her.

It was a family ritual that presents were not opened until after the celebratory birthday tea, complete with cake and candles, which Leigh's two daughters had helped their grandfather to blow out.

Now all the presents had been opened and the girls were arguing over which one of them had blown out the most candles.

'Early bed for these two tonight, I think,' Leigh commented to Debra. 'Otherwise it's going to be quarrels and tears. And no encouraging them to stay awake,' Leigh warned Debra mock severely.

Debra had offered to baby-sit for her sister so that she and Jeff could have an evening out together.

Later, as the two of them were walking companionably back through the village to Leigh's house, the girls skipping ahead of them, Leigh asked, 'You seem preoccupied. Is something wrong?'

Debra started to shake her head and then caught the wry look Leigh was giving her, and admitted instead, 'Sort of.'

Hesitantly she explained the situation which was developing between herself and Marsh.

'So?' Leigh pressed her when she had stopped speaking.

Debra gave her a puzzled look.

'Debra,' Leigh told her in obvious amused exasperation, 'I don't think that many women would consider having a man they're physically attracted to, and who's obviously attracted to them, a problem.

'In fact, most women's worry would be that he *didn't* want them, not that he did.'

Debra flushed defensively.

'I'm not like you, Leigh,' she said quietly. 'I'm not interested in ... in passion.'

Leigh had stopped walking and Debra had to stop as well.

'You mean that you're afraid of experiencing passion, don't you?' Leigh challenged her. 'Debra, for heaven's sake, you're denying yourself one of the most intense and special human emotions there is ...'

'In *your* book,' Debra told her fiercely. 'I'm *not* like you, Leigh. I don't *want* that kind of intensity in my life. It's ... it's so destructive.'

Leigh's face shadowed.

'You're thinking about Paul and me, aren't you ... about our divorce? But, Debra, it was out of Paul's and my desire that the girls were conceived. Out of your so-called destruction...'

Tears clogged the back of Debra's throat as Leigh told her quietly and sincerely, 'It's true that loving Paul, that wanting him caused me intense hurt and pain, but I've never regretted loving him, Debs, and I'd go through ten times that amount of pain rather than never experience the joy of loving someone so completely...of wanting them so completely.'

'But I'm different. I *don't* want that experience.'

'Don't you?' Leigh challenged her. 'Your *mind* may not want it, Debs, but your body, your senses, your emotions are telling a different story, aren't they?'

Unable to contradict her, Debra turned away and started to hurry after the girls.

There was a sharp pain inside her chest. She wished Leigh had never raised the subject. She ought to have known that her stepsister wouldn't understand, but then, as Leigh caught up with her and said gently, 'Everyone's afraid of commitment...of loving someone and of losing them. It's a fear we all share, Debs,' she realised that she had misjudged her.

'*You've* never been afraid,' she responded unsteadily.

'No?' Leigh gave her a wry smile. 'Jeff wants to marry me. I know I love him. The girls adore him...and he certainly loves me and them, but

I can't say yes. I *am* afraid, Debs, but listening
to you has suddenly made me realise how destructive that kind of fear can be, and how
hurtful. It isn't Jeff's fault that Paul stopped
loving me and left me. Because my trust in Paul
was misplaced, it doesn't mean that I can't trust
Jeff.

'You can't make plans for a watertight life,'
she added as they reached her small house. 'It
isn't a column of figures where two and two's
always going to equal four.'

By concentrating on keeping her two nieces
amused and illicitly awake while she was baby-
sitting, Debra managed to convince herself that
she was far too busy to think about Marsh.

But she dreamed about him that night;
dreamed that he was holding her, kissing her, and
that she was clinging to him, pleading with him,
whispering to him to hold her and touch her, her
subconscious allowing her senses and emotions
the freedom to express their needs, which she
denied them in her conscious state.

Fragments of her dreams which had lodged
themselves in her memory came back to disturb
her once she was awake.

She paused, shuddering a little as she brushed
her hair, her reflection in the mirror of the
bedroom which had been hers while she was
growing up eclipsed by the hazy, vague images
surfacing from her dreams.

Images in which she clung to Marsh, her body closely entwined with his, eagerly absorbing its intimacy, her face rapt with passion and desire.

She had never seen herself like this before, never created or felt the need to create this other Debra, her hair a wanton tumble of dark blonde silk, an erotic contrast to the lean male body against which it fell, her own body taut, yearning, trembling in the extremity of her need, and on her skin the sheen of her desire-induced perspiration. Her nipples taut and hard, dark with the blood that pulsed beneath her flesh, but most disturbing and unfamiliar of all was the expression on her face, the taut, shivery urgency of her breathing, the words of need and desire that floated through her memory, incoherent pleas, whispered phrases, things she had never imagined herself capable of thinking, never mind saying.

It *wasn't* real, she reminded herself shakily. It was just a dream. It couldn't happen. It *must* not happen.

'That was a wonderful lunch, but what we all need now is some exercise,' Leigh announced firmly next day.

Debra protested that she was too full even to think of moving, and then reluctantly got to her feet, following Leigh's example.

'Never mind the washing-up,' Leigh instructed their parents. 'We can all help with that when we come back. Let's make the most of the sunshine and enjoy it. We needn't walk very far. Just down to the river and back.'

They weren't the only people taking advantage of the fine weather. The village was a popular beauty spot and a good centre for several excellent local walks.

Debra smiled as she heard a small child exclaiming in awe at the date above one of the shops.

'1590. That was hundreds and hundreds of years ago.'

'Thousands probably,' another child chipped in, while a patient parent started to correct his error.

Leigh's two daughters, familiar with this summer inrush of visitors, were displaying the superiority they felt as local inhabitants, and Debra watched the by-play with tender amusement, unaware that she herself was the object of someone else's observation until she heard a male voice speak her name.

'Marsh!'

Her recognition of his voice was immediate, shock overwhelming caution as she turned round and saw him standing a couple of feet away.

Numbly she took in the casual shirt and jeans, the workmanlike walking shoes and the local map he must have been studying when he'd seen her, and her agitation subsided a little.

How silly of her to assume that he had come here to seek out *her*, when he was obviously here to walk and explore a little of his new habitat.

'Marsh?' she heard Leigh querying interestedly at her side before smiling at Marsh and extending her hand, saying wryly, 'I believe I owe you an apology. A case of mistaken identity.'

'Ah, the lady detective,' Marsh responded.

'I am truly sorry about what happened,' Leigh told him. 'No wonder you were so angry.'

Debra saw Marsh's head turn in her direction. 'A little,' he agreed, 'but it did have its . . . compensations.'

Debra swallowed. Her mouth had suddenly gone very dry. She had an insane compulsion to wet her lips with her tongue-tip; to relieve the dryness which seemed to be making them swell and throb a little.

Marsh was still looking at her. She wanted desperately to look away, but for some reason she couldn't.

She could hear Leigh calling to their parents, 'Come and meet Debra's new boss,' and felt a panicky urge to turn and run before it was too late, but too late for what?

Her mother was smiling at Marsh while Leigh introduced them. She heard Marsh making a reference to her stepfather's birthday. Both men laughed; the sound was mellow, harmonious somehow, as though they had immediately reached out to one another on some special male level which for a brief spell excluded the watching women.

'Have you just finished your walk, or were you just about to begin it?' Debra heard her mother asking.

'I was just about to begin it,' Marsh told her. 'But there are so many walks to choose from that I wasn't sure...'

'Why not come with us?' Leigh suggested immediately. 'We're only walking as far as the river. A pre-washing-up attempt to offset the effect of Mum's Sunday lunch.'

They all laughed... except Debra. She was too bemused, too confused... too filled with a sudden sharp sense of events slipping away from her in some way to do anything other than glance anxiously from Leigh's face to Marsh's.

Surely he couldn't possibly want to come with them? He was dressed for walking; they were only going for a short stroll, but he was already falling into step with them, and somehow Debra discovered that she was walking next to him as they separated into smaller groups to navigate the busy narrow street.

She tensed as he took hold of her arm, steadying her as someone jostled past her. She fought the fierce surge of pleasure that dizzied her, trying to breathe deeply and calmly, looking straight ahead as she thanked him and quickly stepped away from him.

'Do you have any family?' Leigh asked him, unashamedly curious, as they all reached the stile into the field.

'Some. But unfortunately I don't get to see much of them these days.

'My sister is married to an Australian. They have three children. My parents retired out there several years ago. I think my mother had given up on me as a provider of grandchildren.'

'You don't want children?' Leigh asked him.

Debra smothered her instinctive protest. Leigh was like that, inclined to ask the most personal of questions of relative strangers. It meant nothing. It was just a part of her personality.

She held her breath, hoping that Marsh wouldn't snub her, even though she knew that she could never have asked him anything so personal.

'Yes.'

But when she looked at Marsh there was no trace of anger in his face. Instead he was smiling, amusement glinting in his eyes as he told her easily, 'Yes. Yes, I do, but, since as yet the marvels of science have not made it possible for a man to bear his own child, I shall have to curb that desire until I find a woman who shares it with me.'

'I can see that would be an almost impossible task,' Leigh told him, irrepressively grinning at him.

Fortunately he seemed to take her teasing in good part.

'Almost,' he agreed, tongue in cheek. 'It's the glass slippers, you see—they will keep on breaking.'

Later, when they had reached the river, and Marsh was crouching down, pointing out to the two entranced little girls some small trout basking peacefully in the sun, Leigh whispered to Debra, 'You're mad. You *know* that, don't you?'

Debra gave her a confused look.

'You want him, Debs,' Leigh continued softly. 'And I'm damn sure that he wants you. For goodness' sake...life doesn't hand out too many chances like that to turn your back on one. All right, so ultimately there may be pain, but it won't be deliberately inflicted. Not by a man like that, and even if it was...' She stopped speaking and looked at Marsh's crouched figure.

'I'd say that he was a man who knows instinctively how to give a woman pleasure and how to appreciate the pleasure she would want to give him.

'That was one of my biggest irritations with Paul. He was a terrific lover, just so long as *he* was the one doing the loving, but he had to be the one in control, and in the end I got tired of being controlled, even though it took me a long time to admit it.

'Don't turn your back on what he's offering you, Debs.'

'He isn't *offering* me anything,' Debra told her fiercely.

Leigh's eyebrows rose.

'No...I'd say his presence here is making a pretty clear statement of intent.'

'That was just a coincidence,' Debra hissed at her, anxiously checking to make sure that Marsh couldn't overhear what they were saying.

Leigh laughed. 'It's no coincidence,' she told her in amusement.

Debra told herself that Leigh was wrong, but when her mother invited Marsh back to have tea with them and he accepted she began to wonder.

As they walked back she could hear the two men, her stepfather and Marsh, chatting amicably together. Her elder niece slipped her hand into Debra's and whispered that she thought that Marsh was 'really nice', and, from the way her mother fussed over him, urging him to have another scone and flushing as he praised the jam she had made the previous autumn, Debra suspected that she shared her small granddaughter's view.

In fact, he was so at home with her family that he might have known them all years and not merely a few brief hours.

She herself hardly took part in the conversation. She sat silently watching the others, tense and on edge, and yet at the same time in some vague way almost resentful of them for the way they monopolised Marsh's attention, and then he turned his head and smiled at her, and right there, in the comfortable shabbiness of the familiar sitting-room, her heart did a double somersault inside her chest and the dismaying truth hit her.

She was actually falling in love with him!

CHAPTER FIVE

'I BELIEVE we've got a group meeting tonight.'

Debra tensed as Marsh walked into her office.

Ever since the weekend of her stepfather's birthday she had deliberately maintained a distance between them, but Marsh seemed oblivious of it, ignoring it, just as he ignored the way she always carefully physically distanced herself from him whenever he came close to her.

She had seen from his eyes that he was not oblivious to it, though, and a small bout of nervousness shook her now as he added, 'I've got to drive past your place on the way there. Why don't I pick you up? Save us using two cars.'

She would have liked to refuse. The mere thought of sitting beside Marsh in the close confines of his car was a burden she did not want to place on her frail self-control.

She might be able to banish him from her thoughts during the day, but at night, when she had no conscious control, it was a different matter.

She was exhausted by trying to fight off going to sleep and then waking too early, her body trembling, aching. Her mind in turmoil as she tried to deny the desire that tormented her sleep.

She couldn't refuse, however. Her car was in the garage, being serviced, and when Brian had rung her this morning to announce that he had brought forward the date of the meeting because he was due to go on holiday she had called the garage and they had informed her that it was impossible for them to get her car back to her until later in the week.

Numbly she nodded her head, thankful that the strident ring of the telephone meant that she didn't have to do anything other than agree when Marsh suggested picking her up at seven-thirty. As he closed the door behind him she drew in a shaky breath of air. Surely he must be able to see that she didn't want to get involved with him, so why didn't he just leave her alone?

'Haven't you heard?' Leigh had derided her when she'd complained miserably to her. 'Men like to chase. They can't help themselves. It's in their natures, poor things. They're designed to respond to the challenge...if you really want someone to blame, don't blame Marsh, blame nature, and besides,' she'd asked Debra with a sideways look, 'are you so sure that you don't really want to be caught?'

'Of course not,' Debra had denied furiously. 'I don't believe in playing those kinds of games.'

'Who said anything about playing?' Leigh had murmured *sotto voce*, and then amended, 'All right...all right. I know you don't want to get involved with him. But isn't it really a bit too late for that, Debs?'

Debra hadn't been able to answer.

It was certainly far too late to pretend to herself that she was ever going to be able to ignore the way Marsh made her feel. And not just physically, but emotionally as well.

But that still didn't mean that she had changed her mind about his not being the right kind of man for her; about the desire she felt for him not being the kind of feeling she wanted to have for any man.

And yet the thought of never seeing him again, of never hearing him laugh, or seeing him smile, watching the way his mouth curled at the corners, deepening the grooves of humour at either side of it, the way his eyes darkened so disturbingly whenever he focused on her, filled her with anguish and panic.

Hypocrite, she challenged herself after he had gone. You're a hypocrite and a fool. She *knew* he wasn't right for her; the emotions, the desires he aroused in her made her feel afraid. That kind of intensity was too dangerous, too consuming.

She was glad that the case she was working on was so complicated that it demanded her whole concentration and left no room for daydreaming about him.

Her client was divorced from her husband, who had left her for someone else. Husband and wife had run their own small business jointly, and until the divorce she had left the financial affairs of their small company totally in the hands of her ex-husband. Now she had discovered how misplaced her trust had been.

During the course of his affair, while they were still married, he had siphoned funds out of the company, leaving it virtually bankrupt, so that when the divorce came, instead of finding herself the owner of half of a thriving business, the wife had discovered that all she did in fact own was half of the company's outstanding debts.

Her shock, her pain when she had first come to Debra for advice, had made Debra wince. It was plain to her that the woman still loved her husband, that she could not believe what he had done, and, over the months, watching the gradual realisation dawn on her that he had systematically and deliberately ensured his own financial security while destroying hers had been so painful for Debra to watch that she often dreaded seeing her.

That was what could happen to women who loved too much; too intensely.

What could happen, she reminded herself, not what *must*, and women could be just as cruel to men.

What *was* she doing? *Why* was she having these thoughts? So she could sense that Marsh was sexually interested in her. So what? That did not mean that she had to respond to that interest or to return it.

What was it that was making her feel so panicked, so on edge? Marsh's subtle show of interest in her, or her awareness of the strength of her own feelings towards him?

She worked a little later than she had intended, anxious to complete what she was doing, and it was a shock when her office door opened and Marsh came in, reminding her easily, 'Don't forget—seven-thirty.'

It startled her to realise that it was gone six o'clock, and irritation, as much at her own lack of awareness of the time as at Marsh's comment, made her push her fingers into her hair in a brief gesture of tiredness as she told him shortly, 'I'm not a child, Marsh. I *can* tell the time, and I haven't forgotten.'

She saw the smile die out of his eyes and wished that she hadn't been quite so curt. It was as though the sun had suddenly slipped behind a cloud, and she discovered that she actually wanted to shiver a little.

Suppressing such a Freudian physical reaction, she bent her head back over her work, hoping that Marsh would take the hint and go.

When he did she breathed a tiny sigh of relief and then trembled a little as she glanced towards her closed office door, mentally recalling how he had looked, standing there.

There were some men who, when wearing formal business clothes, looked either very ill at ease or so unapproachable that their clothes immediately diminished their sex appeal, and then there were others—a very few others, like Marsh—who seemed so immediately at ease with themselves and their clothes that whatever they wore, whether formal or casual, seemed in some subtle and totally uncontrived way to accentuate their maleness and to bring it sharply into focus so that as a woman one was immediately aware of that maleness.

Sighing, Debra acknowledged that she wasn't going to get any more work done. It was already later than she had realised. She had to clear her desk, to get home, have something to eat, to shower and change and to be ready when Marsh came to pick her up at half-past seven.

Tiredly she stood up, clearing away her papers, locking them in her desk drawer, checking her diary for the next day, just to make sure she didn't have any appointments she might have overlooked, and making a few brief notes to remind herself that she still had to complete the work she was doing on Elisabeth Groves's file.

Normally she enjoyed her short walk home from the office; often she took the longer route, around the outskirts of the old part of the city, stopping to watch the river, and to wonder how it might have looked when seen through Roman eyes.

Leigh had always chaffed her for her romantic daydreaming streak, but in a gentle rather than an abrasive way, and Debra openly admitted that it was perhaps not a characteristic one might normally expect to find in someone who had chosen accountancy as their career. But then she reflected that it underlined the fact that no person was ever one-dimensional, and that no person was necessarily inwardly exactly as they seemed outwardly; that human beings were very adroit at concealing those parts of their natures they considered to be the most vulnerable and at projecting those which seemed the strongest and most powerful.

Tiredly she reflected that she couldn't imagine Marsh having any weaknesses, *any* vulnerabilities, or at least none which he was not totally in control of.

Unlike her. Why *couldn't* she control the dangerous reaction she had to him?

She had never felt like this about anyone before. Never experienced this frightening surge of awareness of how very vulnerable she was emotionally.

Perhaps that was why it terrified her so much.

This evening her walk home failed to soothe her or to distance her from her worries.

She fished her keys out of her bag, unlocking her front door and going inside.

She had fallen in love with her small house the moment she had seen it, feeling as though its smallness somehow wrapped itself protectively around her. She had lovingly decorated and furnished it, spending hours at antiques fairs and house sales, looking for exactly the right pieces of furniture.

Some of her most treasured pieces had been lovingly restored, dozens of coats of paint stripped from them to reveal the richness of their wood, but this evening as she walked through her small hall, the pretty little oak table with the mirror above it and the pair of wall sconces either side of it, which were some of her favourite finds, failed to lift her spirits.

Tiredly she inspected the contents of her fridge, before acknowledging that she was far too nervous to want to eat.

Some fruit and a cup of coffee—that was about all she could manage.

Upstairs she stripped off her office clothes and showered quickly, desperately trying to ignore the treacherous sensuality of her own skin. Had her body always possessed this hidden awareness of its power to respond to the subtle messages of another human body? And, if so, why had she never recognised it before? Why was it only now that she was aware of the silky sheen of her damp skin, of the softness of the curves and hollows of her body, of its shape, its sexuality, of its physical design that was both so tactile and so sensitively responsive to physical touch that its reactions were clearly visible to the naked eye?

Experimentally, angry with herself for doing so and yet somehow driven to test herself, to punish herself, she thought about Marsh, pictured him as she had seen him last, standing in the doorway to her office.

Immediately her stomach muscles knotted and her nipples hardened, a tiny *frisson* of sensation bringing her body out in a rush of goose-flesh and making her stomach churn tensely.

If he were here with her now... how would it... how would she...?

Stop it, she warned herself fiercely, quickly reaching for her towel, as though somehow by wrapping it tightly around herself she could suppress what she was feeling, binding it so tightly that she deprived it of the ability to survive.

In her bedroom, she opened her drawers, removing clean underwear, dressing quickly in her jeans and a cotton top with a round neckline and four small buttons unfastening the front.

It had been an impulse buy, but now, glancing at her reflection in the mirror, she frowned a little. She hadn't realised that the round neckline revealed quite so much of her bare shoulders, nor that those four tiny buttons would look quite so... so... provocative somehow.

She frowned a little, deriding herself that it was only her imagination, her physical awareness that made her think so. Her imagination that furnished her with that dangerous mental image of Marsh leaning towards her, his fingers touching those buttons, his mouth exploring the warm curve of her throat and shoulder.

Her face bright red with temper and embarrassment, she reached for her hair-drier, telling herself that for someone who wanted to keep Marsh completely out of her life she was behaving in a very odd way.

When he arrived at seven-thirty she was ready, her heart beating frantically fast, all her senses leaping into sharp awareness as she opened the door to him.

It was like living life on a different plane, changing into a different and far more dangerous gear. It was an awareness that sharpened and accentuated every single one of her senses and which made it impossible to walk with him to his car without having to distance herself from him.

Once she was actually in the car with him it intensified even further. She felt quite sick with tension, exhausted by the frantic race of her heartbeats and yet at the same time so on edge that she felt as though it would never be possible for her to relax properly again.

'Are you all right?' Marsh asked her, glancing briefly at her as he waited for a set of traffic-lights to change.

Immediately her tension increased. She glanced away from him, hoping that the hot colour she could feel burning her face had not extended to her throat, where he might see it.

'Yes, I'm fine,' she lied, carefully keeping her voice cool and distant.

She could see that he had registered that distancing vocal warning. His face hardened a little, but he made no further comment other than to say how very relaxing and enjoyable he found living in Chester after the faster pace of London and New York.

'But surely eventually you'll have to return to one or other of them?' Debra commented. Her comment was intended to remind her that his time in Chester was limited; that he would not be there for very long, rather than to ask personal questions, but he, of course, could not know that, she admitted as she felt the quick look he gave her almost as though her question, her interest, had surprised him.

'Not necessarily,' he told her. 'I could, if I wished, choose to stay in Chester.'

'But surely the best jobs, the best career moves for you, must be in London or New York?' Debra insisted, suddenly anxious and edgy.

'That depends on how one defines the description "the best",' Marsh said wryly. 'I don't happen to subscribe to the view that the most important thing in a man's or a woman's life must necessarily be his or her career. For me it certainly isn't. It's true that I've enjoyed the challenges my work has given me, but I don't intend to become a man who has nothing else in his life other than work.'

Debra couldn't bring herself to ask him what else he might want in his life.

Because she was afraid of the answer?

'What about you, Debra?' he enquired, turning the tables on her. 'Do you intend to make your career the main focus of *your* life?'

'No.' Her denial was so immediate that she flushed a little in chagrin at what it might have betrayed.

'You want children, then?' Marsh pressed.

'I should like to have a family,' Debra admitted more cautiously. 'But only within the right kind of relationship.'

She was aware that Marsh was looking at her, but she kept her gaze fixed firmly on the road in front of them, while inwardly wondering why she had made that kind of statement. Had she done it as a warning to Marsh or as a reminder to herself?

'Surely there *is* only one kind of relationship that matters?' Marsh queried. 'The kind where two people love one another and want to express that love through the conception of their child.'

Their conversation was becoming too personal, too dangerous, Debra thought, panicking a little.

'Sometimes when two adults...love one another their love can be too intense, too volatile to provide a secure background for their children,' she told him quickly.

Out of the corner of her eye she could see him frown, and she had a sudden quick suspicion that her words might have betrayed more to him than she wanted him to know.

To her relief they had turned into Brian's road, and she said quickly, 'That's Brian's house. That one on the right,' even though she could see that Marsh was perfectly well aware of their destination.

This time she took care to find a chair between two that were already occupied, flushing a little as she saw the speculative assessing look Marsh was giving her.

He was a very intelligent man. Had she said too much, perhaps *betrayed* too much to him tonight? But if she had, surely he must realise that there was no point in pursuing her; that she was simply not the kind of woman who wanted what he could offer?

Not that he had shown any particular interest in her as a woman on the way over here, she reminded herself. She had been the one who had been too far aware of him, not the other way around.

Because everyone seemed to have several points to raise the meeting went on longer than usual.

Debra in particular wanted to discuss her concern over the situation at the home, where one child could bully and frighten another without anyone in charge being aware of it.

He had had an opportunity now to make contact with Kevin Riley, Marsh announced. A faint shadow darkened his eyes as he paused.

'He's obviously having problems adjusting his behaviour to meet the standards that society expects. He's been the victim of an extremely violent and abusive father, and I have to confess that I'm not sure it's going to be possible to eradicate the behavioural patterns he's absorbed from living with his father. He has a tendency to express himself through physical violence. I hate the ideas of pigeon-holing or condemning any child——'

'He's not a child. He's fourteen, going on forty,' one of the others put in tiredly. 'The boy's a thug, and destined to end up in trouble.'

Debra looked at Marsh. His mouth had tightened a little, but she saw from the expression in his eyes that he was aware that there was an element of truth in what had been said.

'Isn't there somewhere he could be moved, to another home?' Debra asked quietly. 'I'm concerned for Karen. She's obviously terrified of him.' She gave a small shiver. 'And I must admit that I can understand why.'

'It can't be done, I'm afraid,' Brian told her. 'There just isn't anywhere else for him to go. Not at the moment.'

It was gone half-past eleven before the meeting finally broke up. Outside, the sky was clear, the stars brilliantly sharp, the air invigoratingly cool after the warmth of the crowded sitting-room.

Marsh made several comments on the meeting as he drove Debra home, but she had learned her lesson, and this time she kept her answers brief and unencouraging.

The street where she lived was in darkness as Marsh drove along it, including her own house.

Debra tensed as she stared at the darkened sitting-room window, where a light should have been shining. She always left the lights on when she was out at night.

'What's wrong?' Marsh asked her, sensing her tension.

'The lights are off,' she told him huskily. 'I always leave them on.'

She saw Marsh glancing at the street-lights as she had done, checking that there hadn't been a power failure, and then he was saying quietly, 'Stay here.'

Debra didn't listen to him. It wasn't up to him to tell her what to do, and by the time he was out of the car so was she, hurrying towards her front door behind him.

It was still locked and they needed her keys to go in, but immediately they were inside she knew she had been right to be afraid.

In the glow from the street-lights she could see the words sprayed on the hall walls, the shattered pieces of her mirror, the deep scratches on her table.

More paint had been sprayed on her carpets, and as she swayed sickly in the doorway, pressing her hand to her mouth, she heard Marsh saying curtly, 'Go back to the car, Debra,' but it was already too late. She had seen enough to know that whoever had broken into her house had not been motivated merely by a desire to steal.

There was evidence here of malice and hatred as well. The house seemed to pulse with a violent energy that contaminated it.

It was Marsh who rang for the police, who explained what had happened, who refused to allow her to go into any of the other rooms until they arrived.

Once they did arrive Debra went through the house with them, shaking off the gentle hand Marsh placed on her arm, afraid of giving in to the compulsion she felt to simply let him take charge.

She had heard and read of the effect that having their homes broken into could have on people, and now she understood how they felt.

The sitting-room was full of feathers from her ripped sofa cushions. More slogans had been sprayed on the walls, words that not merely demeaned her personally as a woman but that demeaned her whole sex.

She saw the way the young policewoman winced as she read them.

Inwardly she was shaking, stunned and sickened by what had happened, not really able to take in the full horror of it.

In the kitchen all her cupboards had been emptied, foodstuffs and broken crockery all over the floor, but it was upstairs in her bedroom that the worst atrocities had been performed.

At first the police were reluctant to let her see in, glancing over her head at Marsh, but she pushed past them and then came to an abrupt halt at what she saw.

It wasn't just that every drawer and cupboard had been opened and her clothes thrown all over the room, it wasn't just the violence that was so frighteningly evident in the words sprayed over her walls; they weren't so very much different from what was downstairs.

What transfixed her was the photograph pinned up over her bed, a photograph of a nude woman obviously torn from some semi-pornographic magazine, the photograph pinned to the wall with the knife that had been used to slash across the woman's body.

Out of the corner of her eye Debra saw that the policeman was picking up her strewn underwear and that it too was ripped and torn.

This wasn't just a robbery, Debra recognised sickly. It was an act of violence, of aggression . . . against her personally. She looked back at the photograph over the bed and her gorge rose. She pressed the back of her hand against her mouth, shaking with shock and fear.

It was well over an hour before the police left. It was Marsh who walked to the door with them, who told them that nothing would be touched, just as it had been Marsh who, when she was asked if there was anyone who might have a grudge against her, had grimly mentioned Kevin Riley's name, something which would never have occurred to Debra.

She was standing in the kitchen when Marsh came back, just staring around, still unable to take in what had happened. The only thing that had actually touched her with any sense of reality was the knowledge that never, ever again could she live in this house; that never, ever again would she feel safe and secure here, that no amount of cleaning or redecorating would ever wipe from her memory the desecration she had seen.

'Come on,' Marsh said quietly, his hand on her arm as he guided her back into the hall.

She let him lead her, numbly following him out to his car and letting him settle her inside it without question or curiosity. She had no idea where he was taking her, nor did she really care. She was still in too great a state of shock, her eyes wide and staring as she fought against closing them and seeing again that violently abused photograph above her bed.

Kevin Riley. *Could* a boy of that age be capable of that kind of violence, that kind of sexual menace? She shuddered, suddenly knowing that he could. Tears filled her eyes and she started to shake.

Immediately Marsh reached out and touched her shoulder, in a gesture of understanding and comfort.

Now there was no room left in her to fear or resent her response to him, only a deep relief that he was there; that she wasn't alone.

CHAPTER SIX

WHEN MARSH stopped the car outside the house he was renting Debra looked uncertainly at him.

'It's almost half-past one,' he told her calmly. 'I didn't think you'd want to disturb your parents so late. I've got a spare room, and the bed's made up. You can sleep there tonight. I expect the police will want to see you again in the morning anyway, and I've given them my address and told them that you'd be staying with me.'

Debra felt too drained to argue. She still couldn't fully accept what had happened.

Somewhere inside her a small panicky voice whispered that she *couldn't* stay with Marsh, but she was too exhausted to listen to it.

Suddenly and wholly unexpectedly she craved sleep, or rather the escape that sleep would bring, and so she stood docilely while Marsh locked the car and then let him guide her up the path to the front door.

He still held her while he unlocked it, as though somehow he instinctively knew how much she needed the security and reassurance of that protective masculine touch.

It was only once she was inside the house with him that she started to panic, remembering that she had no change of clothes, no toothbrush, no personal possessions of any kind, and yet the thought of going back to what had once been her home, to search through the devastation and contamination for those things, made her stomach churn with nausea.

'It's this way,' she heard Marsh saying quietly, the light touch of his hand on her arm guiding her towards the stairs.

She half stumbled on them, her body shaken by rigors she could not control. She heard Marsh curse, a muffled explosive sound that tensed her already strained muscles as her body recognised the male sound of aggression and reacted to it, terrifying vivid slashes of visual memories jagging through her brain: her bedroom, her clothes, that photograph.

She made a small whimpering sound of fear that Marsh instantly picked up on, turning to her, holding her as she turned to run, and then quickly picking her up so that her sharp cry of protest was muffled against his shoulder as he carried her the rest of the way up the stairs.

Distantly her mind registered the fact that her body welcomed rather than rejected him, that somehow being held by him made her feel safe . . . secure.

Her senses welcomed the house's anonymity. If it was alien and unfamiliar to her then he, whoever it was who had destroyed her home and her peace of mind, would not be drawn to it to desecrate it as he had done her home.

Marsh crossed the landing and pushed open a bedroom door, nudging the light switch with his shoulder.

The room was small and plainly furnished—a bed, an old-fashioned walnut dressing-table and wardrobe, a dull green carpet on the floor and equally dull curtains at the window—but Debra welcomed its dullness, its lack of anything that corresponded to the bedroom she had decorated and furnished with such enjoyment and care.

She knew she would never ever be able to walk into that bedroom again without seeing what had been done to it.

'The bathroom's the first door on the left,' Marsh told her quietly as he slowly released her. 'I'm just going downstairs to make us both a drink. Call me when you're in bed.'

'But I can't go to bed,' Debra told him. 'I don't have anything to wear.'

She frowned as she heard the words, not recognising the whispery, confused sound of her own voice, trembling a little as she sensed how intense her shock must be for her to make that kind of comment... for her to actually look to Marsh to protect and provide for her, as though somehow she had reverted to childhood and was incapable of doing those things for herself; she, who prided herself on her independence.

'Wait here,' Marsh told her.

When he had gone she stared round the room, abruptly filled with such a sense of panic that she wanted to run after him, to plead with him not to leave her.

She was actually turning towards the door when he came back, carrying a soft blue shirt.

'I don't wear pyjamas, I'm afraid, but perhaps this will do,' he offered, handing it to her.

It was clean and ironed and yet when she touched it, gripping it with her hands, holding it tightly against her body, her grip seemed to release from its fibres an elusive hint of his body scent.

'Don't worry. You're perfectly safe here,' Marsh told her, watching her.

'You really think it might have been Kevin Riley?'

The words burst from her, filled with need to have him deny it, but instead he said tiredly, 'It seems like it.'

'That means he must know that Karen told me.'

'It's all right,' Marsh assured her. 'The police checked. Karen is perfectly safe. And so are you.'

Debra looked solemnly at him, her eyes wide and dark.

'Am I?' she questioned tautly.

'Yes.' He sounded so sure, so calm, that a little of her fear seeped away.

The bathroom was old-fashioned and rather chilly. In any other circumstances she would have found the rented house slightly depressing, with its lack of those small personal touches that made a house a home, but now she almost welcomed its blank anonymity, drying herself slowly on the rough towel she had found in the airing cupboard, her movements weighed down by fear and stress.

She hesitated before putting on Marsh's shirt, touching it reluctantly before sliding her arms into it and then quickly fastening the buttons. She was just walking across the landing on her way back to her bedroom, when she heard Marsh call out from the bottom of the stairs, 'Debra, are you all right?'

Immediately she tensed, frozen into immobility and speechlessness, caught fast in a paralysing web of panic and fear.

She heard Marsh coming upstairs but still couldn't move. She saw him frown as he looked into her face, distantly aware of the controlled urgency of his movements as he put down the mug he was carrying and came towards her.

The sensation of his arms going round her, of being held and rocked as though she were still a child, swept aside reality and logic. She leaned on him instinctively, soaking up the comfort of his body, its warmth and protection, a child again, seeking the safe comfort of an adult to protect her from her childish fears.

'That photograph,' she said painfully, the words surfacing past the defences she had tried to erect against them. 'He wanted it to be *me*, didn't he? He wanted to do that to *me*.'

She was shaking now, the nausea and fear raking her stomach with sharp nails of terror.

'You mustn't think of it like that,' Marsh told her. 'That's what he *wants* you to do.'

'But if I'd gone back to the house while he was still there...'

She felt his arms tighten around her and her body trembled harder.

'Thank God that didn't happen,' she heard him saying harshly, and then he gave her a small shake, his voice relaxed and easy, even though she could still feel the tension in his body, as he told her, 'Come on. You need to get some sleep. I've put some brandy in your hot chocolate. That should help.'

As she responded to his words and started to pull back from him he held on to her and said softly, 'Think you can make it, or do you want me to carry you?'

To *carry* her. Suddenly the tremor that ran so sharply through her had nothing at all to do with her trauma, and everything to do with the way she was imagining being held in Marsh's arms and being carried by him to bed. Not a single solitary bed, but to a large shared one, where he might slowly unfasten the buttons of her borrowed shirt, laying bare her body to his gaze and to his mouth.

Shocked that she could have such thoughts after everything that had happened, she denied quickly, 'No. No...I can manage,' turning quickly towards her bedroom and hurrying into it, while he followed her with her drink.

'I'll leave the bedroom door open and the landing light on,' he told her. 'And, if you need to, don't be afraid to call out. I'm only a light sleeper. You *are* safe here, Debra,' he added firmly. 'If I thought you were in the least danger it wouldn't be in this bed you'd be sleeping, but in mine.'

The look he gave her made her heart turn over. He meant it, she recognised dizzily, her whole body shaking with an unfamiliar excitement. She moistened her dry lips with the tip of her tongue.

What if she were to tell him that she was so frightened that she didn't think she *could* sleep alone?

Instantly she was appalled and ashamed of her thoughts. Keeping her back to him, she waited for him to put down the drink and leave her.

Super-sensitive to his movements, she heard him pause as he reached the door. The tiny hairs along her spine quivered when he spoke to her.

'Remember,' he told her, 'if there's anything you want or need...'

The only thing she wanted was to somehow blot out her visual memories of what had been done to her home, she told herself as she climbed into the bed. But was it? Didn't she want *him*,

Marsh, here in bed with her, holding her, protecting her, loving her?

No, no, of course she didn't, she told herself shakily. That was exactly what she didn't want. What she could not *allow* herself to want.

She sat up in bed, holding the mug of chocolate, sipping it and pulling a face as she felt the raw sting of the spirit it contained on the back of her throat.

Exactly how much had Marsh put in it? she wondered dizzily ten minutes later. It felt like enough to knock out a horse, never mind her.

She could feel herself succumbing to the strength of the alcohol, her thoughts slowing, easing, her body unable to hold on to its tension as she slid unstoppably into sleep.

She woke up slowly and muzzily, a sour taste in her mouth, her head aching slightly. She turned her head towards the window, blinking in the light coming through her curtains. What time was it? She was still wearing her watch. She glanced at it and then tensed. Ten to ten. It couldn't be. She ought to be at work.

She was halfway out of bed before she realised that all she had to wear were yesterday's already worn clothes. She grimaced with distaste at the thought of putting them on again, especially her underwear.

Marsh should not have let her sleep. He should have woken her. She frowned as her gaze suddenly focused on the green carrier-bag on the bedroom chair. There was a note pinned to it. She frowned as she read it.

Hope these will be the right size.

She got out of bed and walked over to the chair, opening the bag. Inside it was a pack of plain white briefs and a box containing a pretty cotton bra edged with pale pink ribbon, and yes, they were the right size. There was also a pair of tights, and another bag, which she opened to reveal a toothbrush and comb.

Her eyes smarted with tears. There had been no need for Marsh to do that for her, and it made her ache slightly inside that he had.

He must, she realised, have been out and bought these things for her, and brought them into the room while she was still asleep. She felt a slight *frisson* of apprehension touch her at the thought of him seeing her as she slept. Had he seen the way she had curled herself into his shirt, breathing in the scent of it like a child with a comforter? She flushed at the thought that he had, and then told herself firmly that he had probably never even given her a second glance.

She wondered what he had told them at work.

Work! She must get washed and dressed and into the office. Quickly she got out of bed and picked up her new underwear, heading for the bathroom, opening the door without even a second thought and then coming to an abrupt standstill as she heard Marsh say warningly, 'Hang on.'

But it was too late—the door was wide open, and she was standing inside the bathroom, her eyes widening in an instinctive female response to the sight of his naked body.

He was, as she'd imagined, lean and tautly muscled, his skin smooth, adhering sleekly to his bones.

His body hair, though, was softer than she had imagined, fine and dark, almost fluffy where it was beginning to dry, so that she wanted to reach out to see if it felt as tantalisingly soft as it looked.

It startled her how erotic the thought of its softness against the muscled hardness of his body was to her, how much the contrast in textures lured her to explore them with her fingertips.

It took her several seconds to register the fact that he had been drying himself when she'd walked into the bathroom, and that he was now holding the towel in front of his body.

When she recognised that the emotion she felt was not one of relief at his modesty but rather one of disappointment, she flushed vividly.

'*You're* embarrassed!' Marsh exclaimed feelingly. 'How do you think *I* feel? I always thought it was the *woman* who was supposed to do the timid cowering behind her towel, not the man.'

He was smiling, Debra recognised, gently teasing her as he deftly wrapped the towel around himself.

'I...I thought you'd gone,' she explained helplessly, her colour still high.

'I *said* I wouldn't leave you on your own,' Marsh reminded her.

'But you must have gone out for these.'

He smiled as he glanced at the boxes she was holding.

'No, I rang Margaux and asked her if she could get them for me. I also told her that neither of us would be in the office today.'

'*Neither* of us? But——'

'The police will want to interview both of us again,' Marsh told her, 'and I thought you might want to go and see your parents. I'll drive you over there.'

'No. There's really no need,' Debra protested, but Marsh was already reaching past her to push closed the door.

'Have you any idea how very sexy you look in my shirt?' he asked her softly.

His words were tiny darts of pleasure, each one of them anaesthetising her to the danger of what was happening.

'Debra?'

There was a question in his voice that made her shiver in silent acceptance of what he was asking.

She heard the door swing gently closed and then he was holding her, touching her, with such finesse and delicacy that, instead of her feeling alarmed or apprehensive, it was like being enfolded in warmth and safety.

For the first time since it had happened, she completely forgot Kevin Riley and what he had done.

Marsh was touching her, gently kneading her tense shoulders, watching her, watching her mouth, she recognised on a sudden stab of sharp longing.

'You want me to kiss you.'

His hand touched her face, gently pushing aside her hair, his thumb rubbing her skin as though savouring its softness.

Without touching her with his body, he leaned towards her.

'I want to kiss you, Debra,' he told her huskily. 'I want to hold you and taste you, to feel you open your mouth to me and want me.'

Her heart was beating so fast that she could hardly breathe. He was arousing her without even *touching* her, without doing anything other than talk to her. Her body ached for him already, a fierce wanton ache that pushed aside all her reservations and demanded that it be allowed this panacea for all that the last few hours had made it suffer.

She moved towards him slightly, an inch or so, no more, but it was enough. His mouth came down on hers, warm and gentle, savouring the shape of her lips, the softness of their texture with a sensuality that silenced the voice of warning struggling to remind her that this was exactly what she had not wanted to do.

His mouth left hers and skimmed her cheekbone, touching her ear.

'Hold me, Debra,' he whispered. 'Put your arms round me and hold me.'

She did as he asked, marvelling at the satin-smoothness of his skin, trembling as she felt her own body's response to this intimacy with his and then tensing as she recognised how cumbersome, how intrusive, how unwanted the presence of his shirt suddenly was.

'Would you like to take this off?'

Had he read her mind? She looked wonderingly at him, her eyes mirroring both confusion and desire.

She knew he was looking at her, waiting for her response, but she couldn't say anything. Her throat aching with tension, she acknowledged that she wanted to feel his skin against her own and that she was certainly old enough, mature enough to be able to say freely and openly what she wanted, but for some reason she felt as shy and tongue-tied as though she were still a young girl, wanting to be shown how to appreciate her own sexuality, rather than a woman who already knew and understood it.

Tensely she reached for the top button of the shirt, willing herself to take responsibility for her own actions as an adult should, but her fingers were trembling so much that she couldn't even unfasten it.

Her eyes filled with unwanted angry tears, which she tried to blink away.

'What is it?' Marsh asked her softly. 'Have I got it wrong, Debra? *Don't* you want me?'

As she looked away from him Debra saw her reflection in the bathroom mirror. Beneath his shirt the tautness of her erect nipples was clearly discernible.

'You know it isn't that,' she told him huskily, flushing a little at her own too abrupt and clumsy delivery of the words.

He too was looking at her breasts now. He reached out and circled one taut nipple with the tip of his fingers, a surge of colour suddenly darkening his skin as he withdrew his hand from her and asked unevenly, 'What is it, then? Is my timing wrong—is that it?'

She ought to have been able to say yes, but knew that it would be a lie. Against all logic she wanted him now more than she had ever done; the sweet taste of pleasure to wipe out the acid taste of fear?

'I just feel so... You shouldn't *have* to undress me,' she told him with fierce self-anger. 'You *aren't* coercing me... I——'

'Would it make any difference if I said that I wanted to do it?' he asked her and, although he was smiling, she could see that he meant it.

Her heart missed a beat and then doubled.

Unlike hers, his fingers were deft as he gently unfastened the buttons, but once he had them unfastened, instead of removing the shirt he slid his hands inside it, pulling her against him, holding her with one hand while the other cupped her face, his fingers burrowing into her hair as he bent his head to kiss her. Slowly at first, as though he wanted to take his time and savour her, and then abruptly, with a sudden sharp hunger that stopped the breath in her lungs and made her press herself up against him as she returned the pressure of his kiss, eagerly opening her mouth, touching his tongue with her own, stroking and caressing it while her heart thumped frantically at the sharp acceleration of her need.

Now she could feel Marsh's hands on her skin, pushing aside the shirt, as he buried his mouth in the curve of her shoulder and groaned that he couldn't wait any longer to feel all of her against him; that he couldn't wait to stroke and touch her skin, to know its warmth and curves, to taste its silky sweetness.

His words were only an echo of her own earlier desire, and she tensed and trembled, remembering it.

'What's wrong?' he asked her, lifting his head to look at her. 'Have I upset you? Shocked you?'

She shook her head.

'What is it, then?'

He was holding her slightly away from him and as he moved, brushing the hair off her face, his body just touched her breasts.

The sensation that pierced her, darting through her like fire, made her draw in her breath, and suddenly she knew that no matter what happened, no matter what price she might later have to pay, she could not, she *would* not deny herself this time with him.

Even if for him it was merely desire...merely sex? She banished the thought quickly before she could dwell on it, silencing the last of her doubts, drowning them out with the sound of her own voice as she told him truthfully and quickly, 'Before...I wanted to *look* at you. To *touch* you,' she said helplessly. 'I wanted...' She swallowed, unable to continue.

'Come here.'

He looked at her, watching the delicate colour flood her skin, and then said softly, 'Give me your hand.'

Shakily she did so, tensing as he placed it on his towel and then covered it with his own, tugging firmly so that the towel fell away.

'Now you can look and touch just as much as you like,' he told her huskily, 'providing you don't mind me wanting to do the same to you,' and then she was in his arms and he was kissing her with the kind of hunger and urgency she had imagined was something only dreamed up by the over-active imaginations of fiction writers and, what was more, she was responding to him just as passionately.

CHAPTER SEVEN

'ALL right.'

Dazedly Debra opened her eyes. She was wrapped in Marsh's arms, her head tucked into his shoulder, his hand resting on her waist as they lay together in his bed.

She was still breathing a little unsteadily, still caught up in the awe and wonder of the physical pleasure she had experienced, and still a little afraid of it.

She had thought she had known everything there was to know about her own body, about its reactions and desires, but the intensity of the orgasm she had just experienced was way, way outside her experience.

And even more alien to her awareness of herself had been the pleas she had whispered, the needs she had expressed; the things she had said as Marsh had made love to her verbally as well as physically.

Now he was gently smoothing her damp hair off her face, watching her a little gravely as he spoke to her.

'I...we should be at work,' she told him huskily.

For some reason that made him laugh.

'To judge from the sound of your breathing, you have been,' he teased her gently, and then, suddenly sobering, he asked her rawly, 'Have you any idea of just how much I still want you?'

'Show me,' Debra whispered; suddenly, unbelievably, she wanted him again. He read that knowledge in her eyes and touched her slowly, stroking her sensitive skin, his tongue lapping at the damp hollow of her throat, its actions mimicking the far more intimate way in which he had caressed her earlier.

Her desire for him flowed through her in a sweetly slow tide. Hunger and immediacy had been softened, tamed a little by what had gone before, and now she could add to her own desire to touch and know him, the knowledge she had already learned of what most pleased and aroused him.

He too, though, had also learned what pleased her, and very soon she felt the sure touch of his hands, the sensation of his mouth at her breast, slowly caressing the taut peak at its centre, and then, when she quivered in an uncontrollable response to what he was doing, pausing to groan softly against the satin dampness of her body before drawing her nipple back into his mouth and suckling so rhythmically and fiercely on it that she knew what he was doing was as arousing to him as it was to her.

Her fingers slid into his hair, holding him against her body, her soft gasps of pleasure an uninhibited response to his lovemaking.

Before, he had urged her to caress him in the same way, his back arching, his eyes closing, his whole body shuddering in an open expression of his pleasure when she did so.

He had shown her so clearly, told her so vocally not just how much he desired her, but how much it pleased him when she touched him.

She had never realised that a man could be so open, so potentially vulnerable about his needs, and it had helped her to push aside her own caution and restraint; to tell him shyly how much the touch of his hands and mouth delighted her.

But not all the time. There had been moments, sensations so devastating, so overpowering that she had lost herself too completely in them to do anything other than let her body speak for itself.

Now, as his hands spanned her waist and his mouth nuzzled the soft flesh there, as he told her that she tasted of honey and roses, and the husky tension in his voice made her tremble inwardly in anticipation of the strong thrust of his body within her own, she marvelled that she could ever have believed she could deny them both this intimacy; this sharing . . . this loving.

The hand stroking the nape of his neck stilled.

Loving. That was what it had been for her. But for him? In his lovemaking there had been all the things she had ever wanted to find in such intimacy, but he had not actually *said* that he loved her.

But then neither had she said that she loved him.

He made a soft sound of pleasure against her skin, his fingers slowly stroking the inside of her thigh.

A thrill of sensation and urgency ran through her, the swift resurgence of her physical desire overwhelming her ability to think.

She moved closer to him, holding him, whispering to him that she wanted to touch him, to hold him, to caress his body with the same intimacy with which he was pleasuring hers.

She fell asleep in his arms, her mouth still curved in a soft smile of completion.

Marsh watched her for a long time, and then gently tucked her hair behind her ear.

There had never been a woman in his life like this one. In his twenties he had been wary of commitment, of allowing himself to love. He had seen too many of his friends marry young, their relationships falling apart under the pressures placed upon them.

But now...now things were different. Now, with this woman, he was ready to make every commitment there was. But was she equally ready to commit herself to him?

He touched her mouth sombrely. She had wanted him, he knew that, and it had been easy for him to see that her awareness of her own sensuality was very limited.

But wanting someone was different from loving them.

Downstairs he heard the telephone ring.

Gently he eased himself away from her, pulling on his robe.

He went downstairs and picked up the receiver, frowning as he listened to the voice of the policeman at the other end of the line.

They had found the boy Kevin Riley, he was told, but there had been some confusion at the police station and unfortunately he had run off and disappeared. He was ringing, he added, to suggest that Debra should not attempt to return to her house on her own just in case Kevin went back there.

He would make sure that she did not, Marsh assured him.

Soberly he went back upstairs.

Debra was still asleep. Much as he would have liked to spend the rest of the day, and as many days as possible after that, in bed with her, there were things he had to do.

He smiled as he saw his discarded shirt, picking it up. His touch seemed to release from the fabric the scent of her skin. He felt his body's response to the sensual messages it was receiving and groaned under his breath.

This was ridiculous, he derided himself, torn between laughter and disbelief. He was a man of thirty-odd, not a boy who had just discovered the power of his sexuality.

He moved quietly around his room, collecting his clean clothes, and then went into the bathroom to shower and dress.

When he came back, Debra was still asleep.

He had some telephone calls to make. He wondered if Debra kept any clothes at her parents', and acknowledged grimly that she would probably feel unable to wear anything that had been in her own house when Kevin Riley had broken into it, and he couldn't blame her for that.

The boy might have had a poor start in life and been set a bad example by his father, but there was no way Marsh could ever condone what he had done. His mouth tightened as he remembered the look on Debra's face when she had seen her bedroom.

He went downstairs, made his phone calls, including one to Debra's parents to explain what had happened, and to assure them that Debra was safe and that he would be driving her out to see them later in the day.

He then went to make some coffee, and realised when he opened the fridge that he didn't have any milk.

He frowned, wondering whether to wake Debra and tell her he was going out, and then decided that he wouldn't be gone long enough to bother disturbing her.

* * *

Debra woke up with a start. It was light outside, and she wasn't in her own bed. Where was she... what...?

And then abruptly she remembered.

She glanced at the pillow next to her own. Trembling a little, she touched the indentation where Marsh's head had lain.

It had really happened. She and Marsh had really made love, and not just once but twice. She gave a tiny shiver as her brain suddenly leapt into frantic overdrive.

Marsh wasn't with her now. Did that mean that he regretted what had happened? That he was subtly trying to tell her not to read too much into the intimacy they had shared? Not to behave like a callow innocent who believed that making love was the same as *sharing* love; as *giving* love?

She shivered again, knowing that this was what she had dreaded all along; that *this* was the reason she had been so afraid of her own feelings.

She hadn't wanted to love Marsh because she was afraid of the pain of losing him.

She tensed as she heard a sound from downstairs that she couldn't wholly identify. It sounded like something breaking, but the sound was somehow slightly muffled, as though whoever had made it was trying to disguise it.

A tiny thread of alarm jerked at her nerve-endings. She sat upright in the bed, gripping the covers, calling out anxiously, 'Marsh.'

She could hear someone coming upstairs and she called out again, more sharply this time.

The bedroom door opened.

Shock held her rigid as she saw who had come in. She recognised him immediately from McDonald's. Kevin Riley.

The sound she had heard must have been him breaking into the house. Those were her last reasoned logical thoughts as panic filled her.

One look into his eyes told her that he had known she was here; that he had come here deliberately looking for her.

'Bitch,' he told her, enjoying the sound of the word, rolling it round his mouth before spitting it out at her.

'You and that little whore, Karen—you grassed on me, didn't you? Think you're so good, don't you? But you're not . . . you're just a tart, like all the others. Good at it, was he?' he asked, nodding at the indentation on the pillow. 'Made you scream, did he?'

Debra felt the nausea burn her stomach, a sour acid mixture of fear and revulsion and shame as well that she, an adult, should allow this boy to humiliate and terrify her like this.

He was only *fourteen*, she reminded herself, but she could still remember the photograph he had pinned up in her bedroom, the destruction he had wrought, and she dared not look away from him . . . dared not let her glance waver. If she did he might move . . . come over to the bed . . .

She could feel the sweat breaking out on her forehead, the numbing singing beginning in her ears that warned her that she was dangerously close to fainting.

She must not... she must *not* faint, she told herself as she tried to blow out the words he was saying to her, the sickening flood of invective and filth that poured from him, and to her most degrading of all the way he described in the most disgusting language there was the intimacy which she had so recently shared with Marsh.

She tried to distance herself from it, to tell herself that he was simply making assumptions, repeating things he had heard from others, and yet she could not escape from the feeling that he had actually witnessed their lovemaking, that he had somehow been there in the room with them.

Was *that* how Marsh had thought of her? she wondered sickly as she fought to suppress the urge to cover her ears with her hands so that she could blot out the destructive corruption pouring over her.

Did Marsh too think of her as just a body, a piece of inanimate disposable flesh?

Neither of them heard the car pull up outside. Kevin had broken in through a rear window, and so it wasn't until he was inside the house and he heard his voice that Marsh realised what had happened.

He took the stairs two at a time, silent and lethal as a jungle cat, pushing open the door and overpowering Kevin so quickly that to Debra it all seemed to happen in a blur, in the fraction of time between one heartbeat and the next.

'Are you all right?' Marsh asked her tightly as he grabbed hold of him.

She managed to nod, but couldn't look at him. Kevin's words still filled her senses, the ugly picture, mental images he had drawn for her destroying her self-confidence and what she now saw as a naïve belief that what she had shared with Marsh had been as awesome and full of wonder for him as it had been for her.

Even when Marsh had removed Kevin from the room and taken him downstairs she still couldn't move.

She heard the front door open and continued to sit there in a frozen trance while the sickness clawed at her stomach.

Although Kevin hadn't touched her physically, she felt as though he had verbally assaulted her, his destruction of the pleasure she had shared with Marsh worse than the threats of violence that had been made against her.

How could any woman ever know that a man really shared her emotions, that he really understood her vulnerability, that he really knew what it was for her to trust and want him enough to put aside centuries of inbred caution and to allow him the freedom to love her and with it the potential to hurt and degrade her?

Was there a part of all men that thought of women in the terms Kevin had just described?

Had Marsh secretly been thinking like that about her; had he secretly been amused by and contemptuous of the way she had so quickly and so completely succumbed to her desire for him?

Did men, all men perhaps, deep down somewhere inside them, divide women into two sharply separate categories—whores or virgins? Did giving yourself wholly and completely to a man mean a subtle shift in his judgement of you? And if it did, shouldn't that be *their* problem, their guilt, their blame and not hers?

So *why* did she feel that if Kevin had attacked her, had attacked her physically, that somehow she would have been in part to blame because he had found her here in Marsh's bed?

When Marsh came back upstairs and into the bedroom she kept her expression rigidly blank.

'Are you sure you're all right?' he asked her huskily. He was walking towards the bed, and immediately she tensed in rejection.

'Yes, I'm fine,' she told him tersely.

He stopped moving, watching her, his concentration on her making her edgy and nervous. What was he looking for? What did he see when he looked at her? A woman who had given herself to him too easily and whom he now despised?

'Where...where is he?' she asked him, her mouth dry.

'Kevin? I've locked him in the car. The police are on the way. It seems he must have overheard them saying that you were staying here.'

He saw the agitated movement she made and came to the side of the bed.

Debra flinched as she felt his hands on her shoulders. Was it really such a short space of time ago that she had welcomed the touch of those hands, that she had pleaded for it . . . begged for it?

She writhed inwardly in self-torment, rigid beneath his touch, rejecting it.

'I'm sorry. He must have given you a hell of a fright. I should have been here.'

Debra could hear the anguish in his voice and with it the guilt, but she pushed that awareness away. She had enough burdens of her own to bear; she couldn't carry his as well.

'Please don't touch me,' she told him quietly and with immense politeness, the kind of chilly distancing politeness one used to unappealing strangers.

Immediately he released her, his fingers flexing as he stood up.

'Debra——'

'I'd like to get up,' she told him, her glance strayed betrayingly to the indented pillow at the side of her own. 'I expect the police will want to question me, and I don't——'

'You don't want them to guess that we're lovers?' Marsh supplied quietly for her.

There was a huge painful lump in her throat, a misery and anguish she couldn't begin to conquer. She wanted to cry out to him that she could not bear the humiliation of other men looking at her and thinking those words which Kevin had said, but her pride wouldn't let her make that kind of appeal.

'We *aren't* lovers,' she told him. 'We just had sex.'

She saw the colour leave his skin. So he didn't like it either, having something stripped of its softness, its delicacy, its personal intimacy and made ugly and raw. Well, how would he have liked to have been in her shoes, listening to Kevin Riley?

'Debra...'

They both heard the car drawing up outside at the same time.

Marsh cursed under his breath. 'That will be the police,' he told her unnecessarily.

She waited until he had gone before hurrying into the bathroom. Her new underwear was still there, and if she did not have the time for the luxury of the kind of grim cleansing of her body she felt necessary then at least she could shower quickly, and dress in the uncontaminated clothes, which, she realised abruptly, were now all she possessed.

She could certainly never, ever wear any of her others again; the mere thought filled her with such repugnance, such sickness that she had to swallow quickly to suppress it.

She had no make-up other than her lipstick, but the last thing she felt like doing was adorning herself. However, the sight of her pale, strained face in the mirror made her change her mind and wish that she had the benefit of some kind of camouflage to hide herself behind.

The police interview was mercifully brief. She thought she saw the WPC's eyelashes flicker a little in brief awareness when she was asked if Kevin Riley had attempted to attack her and she replied huskily that he had merely been verbally abusive.

Merely verbally abusive. She doubted if she would ever stop hearing the echo of his words.

Before they left the police explained to them what had happened. Kevin had apparently been found in Chester in an amusement arcade. They had taken him into custody, telling him that they wanted to talk to him about the break-in at her house, and they suspected that it must have been while he was either in the car or in the police station that he had overheard someone saying that she was staying with Marsh.

There had been some confusion at the police station caused by an influx of tourists who had come to report one of their number having her handbag snatched, and it had been during this confusion that Kevin had escaped.

'I shouldn't have gone out,' Marsh intervened bitterly. 'I should have guessed that he might come here.'

'How could you?' the police officer asked him. 'None of us had any idea he knew Debra was here. Are you sure you're all right?' he asked Debra. 'Shock can be a funny thing.'

'I'm all right,' Debra told him quickly. He was probably a perfectly pleasant man, but suddenly his very presence seemed to intimidate her.

Was he thinking the same as Kevin Riley? Beneath his surface concern and respect, was he mentally describing her with the same ugly words that Kevin had used?

Instinctively she took a step back from him, unaware of the way Marsh frowned as he watched her.

After the police had gone Marsh asked her quietly, 'Debra, what *exactly* did Kevin Riley say to you?'

'Nothing,' she lied quickly, too quickly, she recognised as she saw the look in his eyes. 'He simply threatened me, that's all. He must have found out that I'd reported him to the supervisor. He knew that Karen had told me.'

Her face suddenly went white... Karen. She had almost forgotten about her.

'Karen?' she demanded rawly.

'She's fine,' Marsh assured her. 'It was probably because he couldn't get to her that he came looking for you.'

Debra said nothing. She knew without being able to say why that he would have done it anyway... that he had enjoyed doing it, and that he had marked her out as one of his victims from that moment outside McDonald's but she couldn't express those feelings to Marsh. She couldn't say anything to Marsh. Not now. Not ever.

'I want to go home. To my parents,' she added quickly in case he thought she meant she wanted to return to her own house. That wasn't her home any more and could never be her home again.

'Yes, of course. I rang them earlier this morning to explain what had happened, and I told them that I'd be driving you over later.'

So even then... he had been planning to get rid of her. He had had what he wanted from her just as Kevin Riley had taunted her, and now he wanted her out of his life. Well, she felt exactly the same.

She wasn't going to allow any man to use her as a means of gratifying his sexuality, no matter how much she might love him.

As he drove towards her parents' house, Debra a silent and somehow hostile passenger at his side, Marsh ached to be able to turn the car round and take her back home with him, but how could he?

How could he criticise her for rejecting him, for blaming him for what had happened? He couldn't stop blaming himself either.

If only he had thought, before so carelessly going out for that milk, he might have worked out for himself the possibility of Kevin Riley's guessing where she was, but he had been so high on happiness and love that he hadn't been able to think of anything else but that love, and how she had felt in his arms, how she had touched and responded to him, how after her initial hesitation and self-consciousness she had allowed him to coax her into abandoning herself so completely and to him so arousingly into her own sensuality.

He hadn't been able to think of anything other than being with her, watching her as she woke up, seeing the awareness dawn in her eyes and then slowly and thoroughly loving her all over again, but now that was all gone, destroyed by his own carelessness.

Of course she must resent him. Of course she must blame him. After he had removed Kevin Riley from the bedroom, all he had wanted to do was to hold her and to reassure her, to wipe from her eyes the glazed, sick look he had seen there, but she wouldn't let him anywhere near her.

She had rejected him totally and completely. It was just sex, she had told him coldly, and, even though he had known she was lying, he had also recognised that there was no way she was going to allow him through the defences she had thrown up against him.

And how could he blame her? He had let her down in one of the worst ways a man could betray a woman. He had told her he would keep her safe and he had not been able to do so. He *should* have been there to protect and safeguard her and he knew he would never be able to forgive himself for the fact that he had not been.

It made no difference that the sexes were supposedly equal, that women these days had no desire at all to be considered as either weak or helpless, and that was certainly not how he saw them. He respected them, accepted their right to define their own lives, and to be treated with the same respect he would accord another man, but nothing could dislodge that centuries-old atavistic feeling that, as a man, he *should* have been there to protect the woman he loved. It had nothing to do with seeing her in any way as an inferior and everything to do with the fact that he loved and cherished her and that despite that he had not been aware that she was in danger.

What had happened to her diminished his own respect for himself as a man, and he was not in the least surprised that she was so hostile to him, so bitter and rejecting.

CHAPTER EIGHT

'ARE you sure you won't stay, just for a cup of tea?' Debra's mother pressed as she looked anxiously from Debra's remote, expressionless face to Marsh's strained one.

Marsh shook his head and thanked her, turning towards Debra, who immediately stepped back from him.

As she saw the look in his eyes she felt her own heart tighten a little in sympathy for him, but Debra was her child and her prime urge was to comfort and protect her, and so she immediately stepped between them, leaving her husband to escort Marsh to the door and to thank him for all he had done, while she gently ushered Debra towards the stairs.

'I don't want to talk about it,' Debra said woodenly when they were alone. 'I just want to forget it ever happened; to put it all behind me.'

Wisely her mother said nothing, but later she voiced her anxiety to Don and to Leigh, who had called round to see if there was anything she could do to help.

'You might try to persuade Debra to go out with you and buy some new clothes. According to Marsh, all she's got is what she's wearing.'

'*Marsh* brought her home?' Leigh asked speculatively.

Immediately Debra's mother shook her head. 'He was so kind to her, Leigh, so gentle with her, and yet it was obvious she couldn't bear him anywhere near her.'

'She's had a very bad shock,' Leigh comforted her. 'And shock affects people in different ways.'

'Has Dr Morris seen her?'

'No. She says she doesn't need to see him; that all she wants is to put the whole thing behind her and to get on with her life. Perhaps you could talk to her.'

'Not yet,' Leigh said gently. 'Let's give her a little time on her own first, shall we?'

'I liked that last outfit, and the bright colours look good for summer.'

'And they might brighten me up mentally as well as visually, is that it?' Debra suggested grimly to her stepsister.

Leigh gave her a thoughtful, clear-eyed look.

'Do you feel in *need* of mentally brightening up?' she asked her gently, and then, putting aside the skirt she had been examining, she came over to where Debra was standing.

'Look, love, I know how hard on you all this has been, and no one can blame you for feeling the way you do, but, well, don't you think you'd feel better if you talked about it instead of bottling it all up inside you?'

Debra shook her head.

'No. No, I wouldn't,' she said shortly.

They had come out this morning to restock her wardrobe. At first she had refused to buy herself any new clothes, wearing the old ones she had found in her wardrobe and in her old bedroom, using the excuse that she couldn't afford to commit herself to that kind of purchase until after her insurance claim had been settled, and her family had allowed her to have her way, even though she had seen the concern in her mother's eyes when she had come down for breakfast for the fourth morning running wearing the same old jeans and sweat-shirt.

But she didn't want to buy new clothes...pretty clothes. People...men seeing her wearing them would think that she wanted to attract their attention; that she wanted them to speculate sexually about her.

Leigh hadn't been as indulgent as their parents, though. She had arrived this morning, announcing that she had taken the day off work and that she and Debra were going shopping, and she didn't allow Debra to refuse.

'Well, you're going to have to buy something,' Leigh told her in exasperation when they had left the fifth shop without her making any purchases. 'You can't go back to work in those old jeans.'

Debra turned her head away. She didn't want to go back to work. Going back to work meant facing Marsh. She knew he had told her parents that she must have as much time off as she felt she needed.

As much time as she needed. Like the rest of her life, and even that wouldn't be long enough for her to forget what Kevin Riley had said to her.

She woke up sometimes in the night, brought out of the deepest sleep by the echo of those words, only sometimes it wasn't Kevin who was saying them, but Marsh.

She couldn't tell anyone about those dreams. Not anyone.

She knew that her family were concerned about her. She was, when she had the energy, concerned about herself. She knew she couldn't spend the rest of her life hiding away from Marsh...from reality, but she also knew that she wasn't strong enough to face either of them as yet.

'Look,' she heard Leigh saying firmly to her, 'either you choose something or I'll choose it for you, Debra.'

She knew that Leigh meant it, and so reluctantly in the next shop they went in she bought a suit and two plain shirts.

'Grey?' Leigh questioned in distaste as they left. 'What on earth made you choose that? It's so dull...so...so anonymous.'

Debra made no reply, smiling grimly to herself. That was exactly why she *had* chosen it.

Leigh paused to admire some shoes in a shop window, chuckling at the height of their heels. 'Heavens, are they back in fashion?' she commented. 'I was wearing a pair of those the night I met Paul, and a skirt that was probably far too short. He told me afterwards that the moment he saw my legs it was instant lust.'

She was laughing, but Debra wasn't. Was that all there was to men's dealings with women...lust...sex?

Leigh was still studying the shoes, her mouth half curled as though some memory they had triggered still pleased her.

'By the way, have you spoken to Marsh yet?' Leigh asked her without looking at her. 'I know he's rung several times... He's obviously very concerned about you.'

Marsh...concerned about *her*? Debra turned on her heel and walked quickly away, ignoring Leigh as she called anxiously after her.

'What on earth was all that about?' Leigh asked her when she caught up with her. And then she saw the brilliance of Debra's eyes and asked more gently, 'What is it, Debs? What's wrong?'

'Nothing,' Debra told her tautly. 'Nothing except that I was stupid enough to have sex with Marsh, and I wish to God that I hadn't.'

She saw the way Leigh registered her words, the momentary shock darkening her eyes.

'I've shocked you, haven't I?' she said flatly. 'Well, not as much as I shocked myself. I've be-

haved like a...with a total lack of self-respect,'
she said harshly.

'But Marsh...' Leigh began uncertainly.

'Marsh just wants to make sure that I know
that what happened between us was nothing personal,' she told Leigh curtly. 'Well, there isn't
any need. I already know.'

'I can't believe that,' Leigh protested unhappily. 'He's been so concerned about you...'

'Because he feels guilty...responsible in some
way.' Debra gave a brief shrug. 'At least that's
what he said. But that's his problem, Leigh. I've
got enough of my own. Like trying to get back
my self-respect. Leigh, I despise myself so much.
Hate myself sometimes...more than I hate him,
even.'

'Him...you mean Marsh?' Leigh questioned
her.

Debra shook her head. 'No. No, I don't hate
Marsh,' she told her in a low voice. 'I meant
him...Kevin Riley.'

She looked away from her sister, unaware of
the frown that was darkening her eyes.

Debra had said almost nothing about Kevin
Riley to any of them, and yet it was obvious from
the passion in her voice that she thought about
him a great deal.

Uneasily she touched her sister's arm and said
gently, 'Debra...Kevin Riley——'

'I hate myself so much sometimes, Leigh,'
Debra told her, ignoring her words.

'Don't we all at times?' Leigh agreed wryly. 'Remember how I felt when Paul first left me? I thought it must be me...that I was solely to blame...that if I had been different...better...prettier, cleverer, sexier, he wouldn't have felt the need for anyone else.

'It's something we women excel at, taking all the blame. It was a long, long time before I was able to accept that Paul was unfaithful to me because he wanted to be. Because the need to indulge his own desires was more important to him than his responsibility to our marriage.

'I know you don't want to hear this, but you must stop blaming yourself. It's a form of anger really, you know. You feel you can't or shouldn't express the anger you have every right to feel openly and outwardly, and so you turn it in on yourself.'

Debra gave her a bitter, caustic look.

'I thought you were a detective, not a psychoanalyst.'

She didn't need Leigh to explain to her why she felt the way she did, she told herself crossly as they walked back to Leigh's car, but later, when she was alone, she found she couldn't dismiss her sister's words.

But if her feelings were not directed at herself then who was their target? Kevin Riley? No, not him. It was Marsh...Marsh, with whom she had shared her most private ecstasy...Marsh, with whom she had let down every one of her barriers, allowing him to see her as no other human being ever had, stripped of the protective layers of restraint and civilisation, the deepest, most intimate heart of her revealed to him through her response to him, just as clearly and vulnerably as his hands had revealed the nakedness of her body.

He had seen her at her most vulnerable, and she had given him a part of herself she could never, ever take back. She had given him her love... herself, and all he had wanted had been her body. And yes, she was angry.

But why should that make her angry with him? Angry with herself, perhaps. After all, he hadn't asked for her love... hadn't wanted it.

And all the time he had been touching her, arousing her, had there in his mind been those ugly, disgusting words that Kevin Riley had flung so tauntingly at her?

She shuddered, dropping her head into her hands, rocking herself to and fro as she tried to ignore the painful demand of her own thoughts.

Was this never going to end...this self-induced torture? Was she never going to be able to forgive herself and start living her life again?

She tensed as she heard the phone ring again. What if it was Marsh again, wanting to speak to her?

He probably just wants to know when I'm going back to work, she had told her mother yesterday after refusing to speak to him.

What was he so afraid of? That she would tell the whole world what had happened between them? Did he realise that she was as anxious to ignore it as he was himself?

She couldn't go back to work, of course. She would have to find another job somewhere else. There was no way she wanted to come into daily contact with Marsh, and he wouldn't want it either.

She went downstairs and asked her mother for some notepaper. Back in her bedroom, she penned a brief, curt note, saying that she felt it best if she did not return to the company and that she would be grateful if her personal possessions could be sent on to her.

She wasn't going back to work, and she wasn't going back to her house. Her mother had mentioned diffidently that her insurance company was having it cleaned up and redecorated, but Debra had refused to listen.

She didn't want to know. She wished passionately that there was some way she could simply wipe her memory clear of everything that had happened . . . including Marsh.

Especially Marsh, she told herself shakily. Especially that.

'Do you feel up to baby-sitting for me tomorrow night?'

Debra looked across the table at her sister.

Leigh had called round on her way to work, and Debra saw the way her mouth tensed a little as she saw that she was still wearing her old jeans.

'I'm not an invalid,' she told her sister.

'No?' Leigh queried grimly, making her flush and say defensively,

'All right, I'll baby-sit. Is it something special?'

'Jeff's birthday. Oh, and by the way, I've brought you this.'

She placed a large carrier-bag on the table.

Now it was anger that stained Debra's face with hot colour as she recognised the name of the clothes shop printed on the bag.

'If I wanted new clothes I'm perfectly capable of buying my own,' she told Leigh angrily.

'Are you? Look, Debs, I understand how you must feel. We all do, but can't you see? I know how hard it must be for you... but you *can't* go on like this. The parents are worried sick about you.'

'And wearing new clothes is going to stop them worrying, is it?' Debra asked her sardonically.

'No, but it might at least lift a little of the burden off them. Unless, of course, you don't want it lifted.'

The accusation made Debra flush and demand reproachfully, 'How *can* you say that?'

'I can say it because I love you and because I care about you,' Leigh told her quietly. 'Debs, can't you *see*, by behaving like this you're letting

Kevin Riley and all those like him win? Is that really what you want?'

Debra didn't answer her, but later she forced herself to examine what Leigh had said and was forced to accept that she was right.

She hadn't realised before the trauma that being a victim could cause, the devastating loss of self-worth and self-respect; the fear that wouldn't let her sleep, and the pain and the guilt.

When she went to baby-sit for Leigh she refused her stepfather's offer of a lift, saying that she would walk and that no doubt either Jeff or Leigh would give her a lift home.

She also wore one of the new outfits Leigh had bought for her, the bright multicoloured cotton suit that Leigh had admired the day they had gone shopping.

When she put it on the bright colours immediately highlighted her strained, colourless face. Grimacing at it, she reached for her make-up.

When she went downstairs and saw the surprise and relief in her mother's eyes she was guiltily aware of the truth of Leigh's comments to her.

'I'll be fine,' she assured them firmly as they both fussed over her.

'Ring us when you get there,' her mother insisted.

It was broad daylight and only a fifteen-minute walk to Leigh's house, but Debra was shakily aware of how vulnerable she felt and how glad she was to get there.

'The girls are both in bed,' Leigh told her, 'and they're to stay there,' she added firmly.

It was only after Jeff had arrived to pick her up and they were on the point of leaving that Leigh turned to her and hugged her, telling her fiercely, 'It's only because I care, you know.'

Then she thought that Leigh was referring to the fact that she had bullied her into wearing her new clothes.

There was nothing of any particular interest to her on television, but Leigh had rented a video for her, and Debra had started watching it before she realised that its theme was a love-story of great tenderness and finesse.

The love-scenes in particular distressed her, but for some reason she couldn't stop watching. Anguish and yearning burned through her as she saw the tender look in the male actor's eyes as he touched his lover.

When she heard the doorbell ring she jumped up in relief, hurrying to answer it.

She opened the door without thinking, assuming the caller would be a friend of Leigh's. The last person she expected to find standing outside was Marsh.

He was inside the house before she could do or say anything, and her body trembled in a mixture of trauma and outrage as she acknowledged how impossible it would have been for her to physically prevent him from coming in.

It was only after she had mastered her initial shock that she realised that he must have known that she would be here on her own and that only one person could have given him that information.

Leigh. Debra smarted as she remembered her stepsister's Judas kiss as she'd left.

'I suppose you and Leigh arranged this between you, did you?' she challenged him bitterly.

'Only because you made it necessary,' Marsh retorted tautly.

Leigh had been reluctant at first to accede to his plea that she help him to see Debra, but when he explained to her that Debra had written, resigning from her job, she had been so shocked that she had given way.

Of his private feelings for Debra he had said nothing, nor of his growing burden of guilt and despair that he had not been with her when she'd needed him.

He hadn't come here this evening looking for absolution, he reminded himself grimly. His guilt was his burden and he must not give in to the temptation to plead with Debra for understanding. Or to beg her for her love?

His mouth clamped in a hard line, and Debra, witnessing the hardness of his expression, felt a flutter of apprehension.

What had he come here for? He must have realised by now that she fully understood the nature of his desire for her.

'I wanted to talk to you about *this*,' he told her harshly.

Dry-mouthed, Debra watched as he produced her letter of resignation, her eyes wide and uncomprehending. Surely she had made it clear enough what she intended?

'What is there to talk about?' she asked him tensely. 'I want to leave the firm. I——'

'You state in your letter that you're giving us a month's notice,' Marsh told her tersely.

Debra blinked at him.

'Yes,' she agreed uncertainly. 'But of course I'm quite prepared to leave immediately. In fact, I'm sure we both feel that that would be best.'

'What we both do or don't feel doesn't come into it,' Marsh told her grimly, and then demanded grittily, 'Did you *read* the new contracts you were given when our two firms amalgamated?'

'Well, yes, but——'

'If you did,' he interrupted her, 'you must have known that it calls for a minimum period of three months' notice.'

Debra swayed dizzily, clutching the door-jamb for support.

Of course . . . of course. How could she have forgotten? They had all been so pleased about that clause as well, taking it as a sign of intent on the part of the larger firm that their jobs were secure.

'Look, I think we'd better go and sit down,' Marsh told her roughly.

Numbly Debra did as he suggested, dropping unsteadily on to the smaller of Leigh's two cotton-covered settees. Marsh sat opposite her on the other.

'You do understand what I'm saying, don't you, Debra? You have to give the firm three months' notice and not one.'

For a moment irritation burned away her shock. It flashed in her eyes, giving her face an animation that reminded him painfully of the girl she had been before.

'I'm not stupid,' she told him acidly. 'Of course I understand,' but then she winced and bit on her bottom lip as she realised that her statement contradicted her actions. Why on earth hadn't she remembered that three-month clause?

'There must be some way round it,' she queried now. 'Some loophole.'

'Perhaps there should be, but there isn't,' Marsh told her, shaking his head in denial. 'I've had a word with head office, and I'm afraid they won't budge. You see, to them you're a very valuable asset. You have a knowledge of your clients and their finances which could not be absorbed overnight by someone else.'

The tension in his voice had changed. He was looking away from her as though there was something, some piece of information he was concealing from her.

Her heart started to race. Could head office be threatening to sue her if she broke her contract?

Nervously she asked him.

He looked rather shocked, surprised, no doubt, that she had guessed he was concealing something from her, she suspected. There was a small pause before he replied slowly, 'Well, of course it's a possibility.'

That meant that they would, Debra reflected.

'I can't come back,' she told him wildly. 'If necessary I'll just have to take three months' sick leave...'

But she knew she couldn't. Her doctor was already making noises about her returning to work, suggesting gently but firmly that too much time on her hands to dwell on what had happened was not healthy.

Marsh's face had lost its colour. He looked as though he was in pain, Debra recognised. She also recognised that he seemed to have lost weight and that his skin had lost some of its healthy sheen...that same healthy sheen which had made her ache so to reach out and touch him, to absorb the warmth of his flesh, its maleness...its strength and its weakness.

That same ache possessed her again, but it was deeper, stronger, now that it held all the power and all the pain of knowledge. Now she knew how his skin would feel, how it would react to his touch, how his muscles would tense and clench and then relax as he succumbed to his response to her.

'You *can't* come back, or you won't?' she heard him demanding bitingly. 'And why can't you, Debra? Is it because of what happened ... or is it because of me?'

She sucked in a shocked breath, her eyes suddenly brilliant and dark with emotion.

He knew the answer already ... of course he did, but if he wanted to drag it out of her, to hear her admit her vulnerability and stupidity, then he could.

'You know that it's because of you,' she told him.

She got up and walked over to the window, keeping her back to him.

'I want you to leave, Marsh,' she told him, hoping he couldn't hear the tears choking her voice.

'Have you been back to the house yet?' he asked her.

His question shocked her. How on earth could he ask?

'No,' she told him fiercely. 'And I never shall. Now please leave.'

She could hear him walking towards her, her whole body went tense and rigid with awareness, but he didn't touch her.

Standing directly behind her, he said savagely, 'You're very good at turning your back on things, aren't you, Debra? Your job...your home...me.'

Suddenly his hands were on her shoulders, turning her round to face him, propelling her against his body and keeping her there while he kissed her with a fierce anger that made her pummel his shoulders with her fists until he let her go.

'I'm sorry. I never meant...'

He looked ill, she recognised, sick and ashamed.

'Get out,' she told him hoarsely. 'Just...just go.'

She could feel the hectic spots of colour burning in her face, but it was only after he had actually gone that she recognised that at no time at all had she actually felt fear; desire, need, anger and even self-contempt, yes; but fear, no.

She walked over to the settee on shaky legs and sank down on to it.

There was something else she had not done either. When she had thought of touching Marsh, of how she had touched him, of how she had loved him, those memories had been completely free of any shadow of degradation, of any echo of Kevin Riley's taunts.

She had, she realised on a sudden sharp sense of roaring relief, never even thought of Kevin Riley at all, only of Marsh...the way he had responded to her, the words he had said to her.

'You're very good at turning your back on things,' he had accused her.

Was she? Was she, as he had implied, a coward, unable to face reality, wanting only to escape from it? Her house, for instance? She might not want to live there again, but it *was* her responsibility. She wetted her dry lips with her tongue-tip.

Tomorrow…tomorrow she would go there… Tomorrow she would prove to Marsh and to herself that, although she might be weak, although she might be vulnerable in her love for him, she was *not* a coward.

Yes, tomorrow she would prove to everyone that she was not a coward.

But first there was something else she had to do which was equally important, and that was to make it clear to her interfering stepsister that she could run her own life.

CHAPTER NINE

'I MEANT it for the best, you know,' Leigh told her remorsefully in a troubled voice. 'He was so very anxious to see you, Debra, and I thought...'

'What? That he was going to take me in his arms and declare his undying love for me?'

Debra's hands clenched as she heard the tears beneath her anger.

She had been stiff and cold last night with Leigh when she had returned home, and had not mentioned Marsh. She had been so hurt and angry that Leigh could have gone behind her back in letting Marsh find her when she was alone and vulnerable that she had not been able to trust herself not to lose control and perhaps even to quarrel irreversibly with her stepsister.

And, whatever else she might feel like accusing Leigh of, she knew that her actions had not been motivated by anything other than love for her.

'So you *do* love him, then?'

The soft question caught her off guard. She swung round, her body tight with tension, her eyes huge, glittering with the tears she would not let herself shed.

'Of course I love him,' she said fiercely. 'But that isn't the point. Do you *know* why he wanted to see me, Leigh?'

Leigh frowned.

'I assumed you'd had some kind of quarrel and that he wanted to make it up.'

'A *lovers'* quarrel, do you mean?' Debra laughed bitterly. 'Hardly. What he wanted to see me for was to tell me that I needed to give the firm three months' notice of my resignation and not one, as I had thought.'

'You're *leaving*? But——' Leigh knew that she mustn't let Debra realise that Marsh had told her this already.

'I *have* to. You must see that. I can't continue to work there. Not with Marsh there.'

She saw Leigh's face, and told her despairingly, 'I might love *him*, Leigh, but he doesn't love *me*.'

'But he was so concerned about you...'

'Concerned to keep me *out* of his life, not in it,' Debra told her with uncharacteristic bluntness. She glanced at her watch. 'I must go. I want to get to Chester before the traffic gets too busy.'

'Chester?' Leigh's frown deepened.

'I'm going to check on the house,' Debra told her, deliberately avoiding looking at her. 'I...I rang my insurance broker earlier and he says that most of the redecoration work has been finished, and I wanted to check on what still needs to be done before I can put it up for sale.'

Strictly, that wasn't the truth. She *had* spoken to her broker, who had seemed surprised and oddly confused to hear from her, but then she could understand why. In the first few days after Kevin Riley had broken in she had refused to have anything to do with any of the arrangements for clearing the house up. She didn't want anything from the house, she had told him sickly. Not one single item from her personal possessions. She couldn't bear the thought of seeing them, touching them, remembering . . . knowing.

She would leave it in his hands to have the place cleaned up and redecorated once the insurance assessors had agreed her claims, she had told him, and until last night she had had no intention of ever going back there again.

Until last night. Until Marsh had so cruelly accused her of being a coward.

'Look, if you'd like me to come with you . . .' Leigh suggested uncertainly.

Immediately Debra shook her head.

'No. I'll be fine on my own,' she told her.

All the locks had been changed, of course, but she had a new set of keys, sent to her by her efficient insurance broker, and these were now tucked safely in her handbag.

She kissed her mother and Leigh and opened the back door. Her stomach was churning, but she wasn't going to back out now, not with Marsh's words still ringing in her ears.

As she climbed into her car the telephone started to ring. Leigh, who was standing closest to it, answered it, her expression changing as she heard Marsh's voice.

'No, I'm afraid she isn't here,' she told him.

The closer she got to Chester, the more nervous Debra became. Three times she circled the end of the street before finally managing to find the courage to turn her car into it.

She was trembling so hard when she parked outside the house that she stalled the gears, wincing at the tortured noise from the engine, stiffening defensively as she looked around, but no one was watching her; the street was quite empty.

As she walked up to her front door she noticed that even that had been repainted and that the brass letter-box gleamed brightly with polish.

The new locks were a little stiff—or was it just that she was shaking too much to turn the key properly?—but at last she got them unfastened and opened the door.

The hall smelled of polish and fresh flowers. She frowned a little over this, and then came to a startled halt as she saw the huge copper bowl of flowers on the hall table, their colours reflected in the mirror on the wall behind it.

The same mirror which she had last seen lying on the carpet in so many tiny pieces, she recognised, unable to resist walking up to it and touching its smooth surface.

The wall sconces had been repaired as well. And, where the walls had dripped paint as bright as any blood, they were now smoothly papered, the paper exactly the same as the one she had chosen with such care and pleasure.

In fact, she realised as she looked around, everything was just as it had always been.

Apart from the flowers. She frowned a little over those, wondering if her insurance broker had arranged for them, perhaps to add a homey touch to the house's emptiness, to woo prospective buyers. But the house wasn't up for sale as yet.

She walked slowly into her sitting-room. Here, as in the hall, everything had been restored and replaced exactly as it had originally been, but here too there were flowers, a large jug of them in the hearth and then a slightly smaller display on the round table behind the settee.

And they must have been freshly delivered, she reflected as she touched the petals of the massed arrangement of sweet peas, because these were still slightly damp.

Slowly she made her way to the kitchen, pausing only briefly at the foot of the stairs as she walked past them, trying to ignore the sudden surge of panic that hit her stomach.

The bedroom. Could she really face going up there?

She fiddled with the flex of the kettle, a new one, but exactly like her old one. As she glanced through the window she saw that the plants in her terracotta pots were enjoying the sunshine, opening their petals to it. She frowned a little as she recognised that someone must have been watering and feeding them for them to look so healthy. Her insurance broker had obviously gone to a great deal of trouble.

She must thank him, she recognised absently as she marvelled at the way even the plates on the dresser had been replaced in their original positions.

Somewhere in the distance the wail of an ambulance siren broke the silence.

The sound made Debra blink. She had dreaded coming back here so much, feared to do so because she had been so convinced that, no matter how much clearing up had been done, she would still see and smell the filth with which Kevin Riley had desecrated it.

And yet now, standing in her kitchen, breathing in the smell of fresh paint, looking through the window to the peaceful scene outside, it seemed as though that violence, that ugliness could never possibly have happened.

But she still had to go upstairs.

Shivering a little, she walked back into the hall. The scent of the flowers seemed stronger now.

She paused to study them, sharply aware of the stairs behind her and of the dread clogging her throat and racing her heart.

Her hand trembled as she placed it on the banister. The wood was smooth and warm beneath her fingertips.

Slowly she walked up the stairs, tensing a little as one of them creaked slightly under her weight.

At the top she stopped.

All the doors were open, as though somehow someone had left them like that deliberately, so that there were no secrets, no hidden dangers.

Her own bedroom door was the nearest, but she went into the spare room first, exhaling jerkily as she studied its clean prettiness.

Like the kitchen, the bathroom had been restored exactly as though she were still living there, right down to her favourite shower gel and toiletries.

All that was left now was her bedroom.

She took a deep breath and closed her eyes, opening them again, quickly afraid of the mental visions her memory might conjure up. She had gone this far. Wasn't that enough? she asked herself. Marsh had said nothing about her going in every room. Hadn't the mere fact that she was *here* proved that he was wrong?

To others, perhaps, but not to herself, she acknowledged shakily.

She walked jerkily into the bedroom and then came to in an immediate shocked halt, the breath leaving her lungs as though she had been punched.

Where downstairs everything was as it had always been, here in her bedroom *nothing* was the same.

On the wall where her bed-head had been, where that awful, terrifying photograph had been, there were now fitted hand-painted wardrobes, pretty feminine ones with glass doors and soft fabric curtains behind them.

The bed was now facing the window, the sun pouring in, to highlight the soft peaches and creams of the intricately quilted bedspread.

Her furniture, the pretty little desk and chest were still there; and so were her other small treasures; the silver-back hairbrushes; the pretty antique jars with their silver tops.

The fabrics, the colours, her personal things, all these were just as they had always been, but the room itself was completely different; so different that surely only someone who knew her, really knew her and understood her feelings, could possibly be responsible for those changes.

Leigh perhaps. Her mother. Her heart ached suddenly with the burden of her own guilt. She had not been the easiest person to live with since the break-in, and she certainly didn't deserve the consideration, the thoughtfulness, the *love* she was witnessing here in this room.

She moved towards the bed, touching the quilt where the sun was on it. It felt warm and soft, and then abruptly a small sound registered in her awareness, shocking her whole body into terrified, frozen immobility.

Someone was coming up the stairs. She had heard that betraying stair creak. Someone was in the house with her.

She opened her mouth to scream, but her vocal cords were paralysed with fear.

She saw his shadow before he came into the room and she started to shake, her body convulsed with violent spasms of terror.

'Debra...Debra! It's all right. It's me... Marsh.'

Marsh.

She stared at him, watching him run towards her, feeling the hard warmth of his hands as he held her, feeling the heat coming off his body, seeing the emotion in his eyes, and yet somehow it was almost as though she wasn't there inside the body that felt these things at all, but rather that she was standing outside it, watching its reactions with detached curiosity, wondering at the strength of the emotion that shook and convulsed her.

'You're all right. It's all right,' Marsh was saying huskily to her, still holding her. 'I'm sorry; I should have thought, but I saw your car outside. You shouldn't have come here by yourself.' His voice was rough now, making her flinch slightly.

'How...how did you get in?'

Her voice sounded dry and harsh, the words unevenly spaced and formed.

She had locked the door, hadn't she... *hadn't she?*

'I've got a key,' Marsh told her absently. 'I've been calling round most days to check that...'

He stopped suddenly, his face flushing slightly, and instantly Debra knew.

It wasn't her insurance broker who was responsible for this careful, caring restoration of her house... her home. It was Marsh.

'You... you did all this?'

He didn't attempt to deny it.

'It was the least I could do,' he told her gruffly.

'But why?' Debra asked him. 'Why?'

Her heart was beating painfully fast, her breathing suddenly uncomfortably constricted.

'Why?'

He gave her a self-derisive smile.

'Because I love you, of course.'

'You *love* me?'

He must have caught the wonder that mingled with her disbelief, because, as he released her and started to step back from her, he suddenly tensed and looked at her.

'It was never "just sex" for me, Debra. Not before, not after, and certainly not during,' he told her roughly.

'But you never said... You let me...'

Her pain was mirrored in her face and in her voice as she raised her eyes to meet his.

'What could I say, after the way I'd let you down?'

He saw that she was starting to frown, and told her brusquely, 'I should have been with you, Debra. When he broke into my house *I* should have been there to protect you.'

The anguish in his voice startled her, but it was the sight of the tears shining in his eyes that really shocked her, moving her to a totally unexpected protective compassion. She touched his shoulder gently, her eyes soft and warm.

'It wasn't your fault,' she told him.

'No.' His mouth twisted bitterly. 'That wasn't what you thought at the time, was it? Oh, I saw the way you felt . . . the way you rejected me.'

'Not because you weren't there!' Debra told him, horrified that he should think that.

He went very still, his eyes dark and bright with self-contempt.

'No? Why was it, then?' he demanded harshly.

For a moment Debra couldn't speak. Her own eyes were shadowed as the memories swept down on her, degrading, frightening memories of words, phrases, descriptions that had destroyed her joy in her own sexuality.

How could she describe those things to Marsh? How could she tell him?

'I love you,' he had said, and she had seen, felt, that he meant it. She hadn't wanted him to love her and she had certainly not wanted to love him. She had been afraid of that love, resenting and rejecting it, and yet now suddenly she knew that it was more important to her than anything else in the world; that *he* was more important to her... Much more important than her own fears; than anything Kevin Riley might have said or done.

She was still touching his shoulder. She smoothed her fingers against it in a brief gesture of comfort and love.

'It was because of Kevin Riley,' she told him unsteadily. 'Because of the things he said.'

She looked up at him, her gaze direct and steady.

'It was as though he had been in the room with us when you... when we... It was as though suddenly all men must share his thoughts, his feelings... as though the words, the way he described us... our intimacy was the way that *you* must think and feel about me.'

She saw his expression and appealed, 'No... please let me finish. I felt so degraded, so sickened... so... so dirty somehow. I couldn't bear the thought that you saw me like that. As a body... anatomical parts... a piece of flesh to be used and then discarded, despised. I told myself it was my own fault... that *I* had known right from the start that I mustn't get involved with you... that I mustn't love you.'

She felt him flinch and told him huskily, 'I was afraid, you see... I've always been afraid of loving someone too much... I thought I'd seen how intensely Leigh loved and how badly she got hurt. There was a boy at college I thought I loved . . . later I realised I had never really loved him at all, but it made me afraid, because I knew that I too could one day love like Leigh . . . too intensely, too demandingly, and so I told myself that when I was ready to marry I'd find a man I could like rather than love, a friend rather than a lover . . . I didn't want *my* marriage to be like Leigh's. I didn't want to suffer the way she suffered when Paul left her.

'You were right to call me a coward,' she told him huskily.

'No. No, I wasn't.' He was holding her now, cradling her, rocking her soothingly, his voice thick with emotion. 'I thought it was just me. That you didn't want me. I couldn't see beyond my own egotistical needs. I didn't even try to see past them. I loved you . . . wanted you, and deep down inside some part of me was furiously angry with you because you didn't love me in return.

'I'm so sorry about Kevin Riley. Oh, God, Debra, I'm so sorry.'

He was still holding her as carefully as though she were a piece of fragile china, she recognised, his body aligned slightly away from hers as though he was afraid of touching her sexually.

As she looked into his eyes she saw that he was afraid of doing so, that what she had told him had made him afraid of touching her, that his love for her was so great that he *wouldn't* touch her, she recognised.

It was in this bedroom that she had first dreamed of him...that she had first imagined him as her lover, even if she had fiercely tried to deny those needs. This bedroom, which Kevin Riley had desecrated and destroyed, just as he had tried to destroy her, but out of love for her Marsh had created this haven of peace and warmth from that destruction.

Out of *love* for her.

'Make love to me, Marsh,' she whispered shakily.

He frowned as he looked at her, his body suddenly tense.

'You don't have to do this, you know,' he told her harshly. 'I love *you*...'

'I need to do it,' she told him calmly, and then added a little less calmly, 'I *want* to do it... I want *you*.'

She was already stepping back from him, unfastening the buttons of her blouse, her heart thumping frantically while her stomach tensed in knots of anxiety and apprehension.

'Debra,' Marsh protested rawly.

She ignored his protest.

'Undress me, Marsh,' she begged him shakily. 'Please undress me.'

He was hesitant at first, pausing, watching her, his face set and grave.

She took hold of his hand, lifting it towards her body, watching the sudden darkening of his colour, her heartbeat quickening as his fingers brushed briefly against her skin.

'Please. Marsh.'

His touch was careful, clinical almost, the silence thick with tension. She could see the pain and regret in his eyes as he slowly removed her clothes, his movements almost leaden and unwilling.

This wasn't what she wanted, Debra realised helplessly. This wasn't how it should be between them. Her eyes filled with tears as she remembered the way he had first made love to her.

'Marsh, what is it?' she demanded in anguish. 'Don't you *want* me?'

'Not want you?' He caught hold of her, pulling her against his body so that she could feel his arousal.

'Of course I want you, but don't you think I *know* how you must feel? How you must dread...?' He swallowed, his throat working, his hands clenched at his sides as he released her.

'What I feel is that I want you,' Debra told him unsteadily. 'I want to touch you, to look at you; to feel your skin against mine. What I *feel* is that I ache inside for you; that my breasts ache for the touch of your hands and your mouth, that my hands ache to touch you. What I *feel* is that I love you.'

He moved then, holding her, his hands cupping her face, sliding into her hair while he kissed her, starved, famished kisses that burned her skin and made her cling helplessly to him, tugging his shirt free of his trousers so that she could slide her hands over his skin.

He tried to be careful, cautious, but she wouldn't let him, swamping his restraint with her own passion; with the tender touch of her hands on his body, with her mouth, until he cried out in torment and reached for her.

She kept her eyes open, absorbing with pleasure the contrast of his darker flesh against her own; the way their bodies fitted so perfectly together, the way the sun dappled their skin, loving the way the scent of their loving filled her senses.

She cried out as she climaxed, straining to hold on to him, to absorb every smallest sensation of pleasure. His sweat soaked her skin, dampening her fringe and misting her eyes, so that the softly painted wardrobes were a warm peach haze.

Deliberately she focused on them, projecting against them her mental images of their entwined bodies, of their personal and private joy.

'I love you...I love you so much,' Marsh groaned.

She smiled as he kissed her, and then whispered in his ear, 'I love you too.'

She knew she would never forget what Kevin Riley had done, but she knew now that she would never be haunted by it either.

Here in Marsh's arms she had found the truth; had seen, felt... heard... known just how much he loved her.

He was right, she *had* been a coward. Afraid of loving and of being loved, but she wasn't any more.

'Are you sure you're feeling all right?' he asked her anxiously now as he held her. 'This room... the memories...'

She shook her head, touching her fingers to his jaw, and then kissing him.

'The bad memories are gone,' she told him truthfully. 'In future whenever I think of this house, this room, I shall think of you and me together here, of you wanting me... loving me.'

'Mm...' Lazily he stroked the curve of her throat with his tongue and then gently bit her.

'Still, it wouldn't do any harm just to make sure, would it?' he suggested throatily.

Debra looked at him and then flushed, her eyes brilliant with laughter and desire as she realised what he meant.

'Again... Are you sure you've got the... energy?' she teased him, her fingertips stroking through the soft hair on his chest, loving the feel of it against her skin, her whole body unknowingly provocatively languorous.

'Oh, yes, I've definitely got the energy,' Marsh told her softly. 'Very definitely!'

'When I grow up I'm going to marry someone like Marsh.'

Bryony gazed scornfully at her younger sister. 'You don't know who you're going to marry,' she told her, adding, 'You might not even get married.'

'Yes, I will,' Sally retaliated quickly. '*And* I'm going to have a dress just like Debra's.'

Both of them looked across to where their aunt was standing with her new husband. They were so engrossed in one another that they might have been alone rather than surrounded by family and friends.

'Happy?' Marsh asked, kissing Debra. 'No dark memories?'

'Only one,' Debra told him soberly.

Immediately he tensed and frowned, leaning protectively towards her. 'Debra . . .'

'Why did that woman from the London office spend so much time with you that day when she came down from London with those papers?' she asked mock seriously, smiling at him.

Immediately he relaxed.

'So, jealous, were you?' he teased her.

'Certainly not. Remember, *I* thought you were a philanderer chasing after dozens of different women.'

'And I thought *you* were the most beautiful, the most desirable woman I had ever seen,' Marsh whispered huskily to her. 'And the most infuriating. I didn't know whether to shake you or kiss you, you made me so angry.'

'Mm. I wonder what would have happened if you'd shaken me.'

'Don't,' Marsh advised, his voice deepening as he told her, 'Believe me, there really was no contest. And, if I hadn't kissed you *then*, sooner or later...'

'Come on, you two, I want to take a photograph,' Leigh interrupted them, but neither of them had heard. They were too intent on one another.

'Oh, well, perhaps later,' Leigh murmured good-humouredly, grinning to herself as she heard Sally remarking, awestruck, to her elder sister,

'I didn't know people could keep on kissing for such a long time, did you?'

'Course I did,' Bryony told her scornfully. 'That's what people in love are always doing.'

'But how *do* they do it?' Sally demanded plaintively.

'Well, I suppose they just have to take a deep breath and hold it...like when you go swimming.'

Behind her Leigh heard Jeff asking whimsically, 'I don't suppose you feel like taking a deep breath, do you, Leigh?'

'Why?' she asked him mock innocently. 'Do *you* want to go swimming?'

'Well, despite all those protests about not wanting love or passion in your life, you don't seem to have any regrets,' Leigh teased Debra half an hour later as she helped her to get changed into her going-away outfit.

'I was wrong,' Debra told Leigh sincerely. 'I *was* afraid. I thought security was more important than love, but now I know.' She paused, struggling for words, and then said shakily, 'It's a bit like being afraid of deep water, isn't it, but all you need to do is to take a deep breath and...? What are you laughing at?' she demanded indignantly as her stepsister collapsed in gales of laughter.

'Nothing,' she assured her. 'Just remind me some time to give you Bryony's description of how "grown-ups" kiss.'

Soberly she reached out and hugged Debra, telling her quietly, 'It won't be the way it was with me and Paul for you, Debra. Marsh isn't like Paul. You can *trust* him as well as love him.'

'I know that,' Debra told her huskily, returning her hug. 'I *know* that.'

Next Month's Romances

Each month you can choose from a wide variety of romance with Mills & Boon. Below are the new titles to look out for next month, why not ask either Mills & Boon Reader Service or your Newsagent to reserve you a copy of the titles you want to buy — just tick the titles you would like and either post to Reader Service or take it to any Newsagent and ask them to order your books.

Please save me the following titles:	Please tick	√
RIDE THE STORM	Emma Darcy	
A DAUGHTER'S DILEMMA	Miranda Lee	
PRIVATE LIVES	Carole Mortimer	
THE WAYWARD WIFE	Sally Wentworth	
HAUNTING ALLIANCE	Catherine George	
RECKLESS CRUSADE	Patricia Wilson	
CRY WOLF	Amanda Carpenter	
LOVE IN TORMENT	Natalie Fox	
STRANGER PASSING BY	Lilian Peake	
PRINCE OF DARKNESS	Kate Proctor	
A BRIDE FOR THE TAKING	Sandra Marton	
JOY BRINGER	Lee Wilkinson	
A WOMAN'S LOVE	Grace Green	
DANGEROUS DOWRY	Catherine O'Connor	
WEB OF FATE	Helena Dawson	
A FAMILY AFFAIR	Charlotte Lamb	

If you would like to order these books in addition to your regular subscription from Mills & Boon Reader Service please send £1.70 per title to: Mills & Boon Reader Service, P.O. Box 236, Croydon, Surrey, CR9 3RU, quote your Subscriber No:...
(If applicable) and complete the name and address details below. Alternatively, these books are available from many local Newsagents including W.H.Smith, J.Menzies, Martins and other paperback stockists from 6th November 1992.

Name:...

Address:...

....Post Code:.........................

To Retailer: If you would like to stock M&B books please contact your regular book/magazine wholesaler for details.

You may be mailed with offers from other reputable companies as a result of this application.
If you would rather not take advantage of these opportunities please tick box ☐